DRAGON BONES

THE NIA RIVERS ADVENTURES BOOK 1

INES JOHNSON

THOSE JOHNSON GIRLS

For Jasmine,
who believed in us.

Love,
Nia and Ines

Dirt was a curious thing. It reclaimed the dead to cultivate new life. It buried dark secrets that later uprooted long-held truths. It entombed the mundane and turned it into a shrine that the living come to treasure.

It also had a nasty habit of leaving permanent stains on expensive linen.

No matter how lightly I moved through the mud-caked forest floor, tiny splotches of mud splattered my linen top. Of course, I knew better than to wear a $129 linen blouse in the Amazon. But this trip had been unplanned, and I hadn't had time to repack for the rainforest. I was supposed to be getting an expensive mud bath in a European spa. Instead, I was deep in the Honduran jungle, where the mud treatment came free.

My boot sank ankle-deep into thick, rich brown mud, and I cursed as I yanked it out. The moist earth splattered thumb-sized droplets on my jeans and forearms. My entire outfit was ruined.

I made my living in ruins like these all over the world—trekking through remote lands in the desert heat, wading through murky swamps, and hiking into bitterly cold mountains.As an archaeologist, I loved what I did for a living. But working with dirt and death all day made a girl wish for fine, clean things every once in a while.

Unfortunately, my arrival at a spa resort would be delayed by at least another few days—longer if I didn't stop the imminent disaster about to befall my current job site.So I shook as much mud from my boots as I could, wiped the dirt stains from my pants, and pretended the Honduran heat was a sauna and my skin was getting a five-star treatment from the soil.

Of course, the mind trip didn't actually work. But it helped me reach my destination faster.

When I finally reached the dig site, I saw the tips of artifacts peeking through the dirt like vegetables ripe for the picking. This job had been an easy one.

These ancient treasures wanted to be found. They reached up from their graves, waving a white flag of surrender for all to see.

But that was part of the problem. There were people who didn't want these treasures found. People who'd rather see them buried again, or even destroyed. Worse, there were others who wanted to pluck this bounty from the ground for profit. The latter issue is what had me picking up my pace, but the former stopped me in my tracks.

I stepped back as a military convoy pulled into the site. A flag featuring five cerulean stars centered in a triband of blue and white was proudly displayed on the sides of the jeep. It was the national flag of Honduras. The indigenous people of this country had their independence taken from them and their identity reshaped by conquerors from another land.

It took centuries for the people to regain their autonomy and reclaim their unique voice. The military might before me showed that they had no intentions of stepping back in time. Which was ironic since this new threat came from the past.

We stood at what was once the center of the *Ciudad Blanca*, the White City, also known as the Lost City of the Monkey God. A giant statue of a monkey lay on its side with dirt covering its lower half. It looked like the ancient people had tucked the statue of their idol under a blanket before abandoning the city. This buried city contained an ancient civilization that had thrived over a thousand years ago. Today, their aged belongings were calling to us to make their voices heard by the masses once more.

Before anything could be taken from the site for further observation, the ground needed to be truthed and then the artifacts authenticated. That was where I came in. An archaeological ground site was truthed when an acknowledged expert—like me —laid eyes on it. Step one, accomplished. Now it was on to the harder, steeper step two, which was authenticating the artifacts. My specific role as an antiquities expert on the grounds of this rare find was to date the findings and prove their authenticity.

The Honduran government believed—hoped— the lost city was only a few hundred years old. Of course they would. The officials were the direct descendants of the Maya. Tourism for the Mayan ruins was big business. History books were only ever written by the victors. If it was found that there had been a civilization more advanced or older than the Maya, it would be a huge problem.

Unfortunately for the government, dirt didn't lie.

What I found was not only older than the Maya, it was also more than a city. This site was vast. From my estimation, these few acres that were roped off were only the beginning. The layout of the ruins that surfaced appeared to be a few blocks of one city in a network of cities.

I walked along the roped-off areas of the site, watching my colleagues go about the meticulous work of unearthing the past. Professor Aguilar of the National Antiquities Coalition of Honduras gently brushed the dry dirt off a dark stone artifact to reveal the carvings of what appeared to be a jaguar head with the body of a human. We'd found many such depictions on the unearthed artifacts—were-monkeys, were-spiders, were-birds.

Professor Aguilar's eyes widened in delight. A second later, they clouded with concern as he looked around at the uniformed soldiers patrolling the site. The writings on the artifact below the were-jaguar were not the hieroglyphs of the Mayan Indians, who were the oldest civilization of record in the nation. This was something older, something that predated the glory of the Maya, something that could rewrite the national identity of a whole country—one that had fought hard to regain its culture, its country, and its character from conquistadors.

They were words I understood, having spoken them recently to two of my best girlfriends who just so happened to be were-jaguars. Luckily, they hadn't caught word of this dig or our next girls' night would be ruined. I needed to keep it that way.

Aguilar's lips pressed together in a slight grimace as he gazed up at the military might encroaching on this cultural dig. A soldier approached. Aguilar hesitated but, in the end, handed over the artifact. The official covered the artifact with a cloth and walked off.

Aguilar's gaze caught mine, and he gave a slight shake of his head. I knew he shared my concerns. The site was a spectacular find. It was one that should be shared with the world, not shunned and silenced like embarrassing, unwanted relations.

As the archaeological team unearthed the finds, the squad of Honduran Special Forces soldiers packed them up and loaded them into the backs of their convoys. I watched the soldiers usher the artifacts onto a truck. They could try to hide the truth, but the coverup wouldn't last long. It had taken a thousand years for this story to come out. It would resurface again. The past always did.

Maybe sooner rather than later. I looked over my shoulder, remembering the soldiers weren't my current concern. A larger threat was on its way. I turned and marched purposefully to the man in charge.

"Lieutenant," I called out. "May I have a word?"

Lieutenant Alvarenga turned stiffly in his fatigues. His raised eyebrows lowered as his lips spread in a proprietary grin. "There's our little Lara Croft."

I tried not to rankle at the comparison, although I didn't mind being compared to her physically. Being compared to either the video game character or the film character portrayed by Angelina Jolie was a compliment, though I was far from a carbon copy.My thick, dark hair was pulled in a loose ponytail, not a long, single braid, and I had wide, cat-like eyes with a pronounced tilt that pointed to Asian heritage. I shared the same regal nose that hinted at ancient Gallic ancestors. My lips were lush and full, calling to an African patronage. My toasty skin tone placed me somewhere between the north of Africa and the south of Spain. And, yeah, I could rock the hell out of tight pants, a tank top, and a fine pair of boots with a sturdy stem.

But that was where the comparison between the fictional character and me ended. Croft robbed tombs and stole artifacts. I, on the other hand, found what was once lost and then shared my findings with the world.From a moral standpoint, we couldn't be more different.

"You never told me, Nia," the lieutenant said as he invaded my space. "Are you a Ms. or Mrs.?"

"I'm a doctor," I said, holding my ground. "Dr. Nia Rivers."

Alvarenga had a foot on me, but I didn't scare easily. Unfortunately, he seemed to be the type who liked that.

"It still amazes me how you arrived on-site so quickly," he said, his eyes narrowing, his smile fake. "And only days after official orders sent my troops and me here."

My eyes were wide with false innocence. "The IAC sent me to ensure there would be no damage done to a potential historical site."

That wasn't exactly the truth. The International Antiquities Coalition, who I often did freelance work for, didn't *send* me. I had alerted them to the site after I got wind of it through a darknet site frequented by fortune and treasure hunters—tomb raiders. I told the IAC I was on my way, and they'd simply pushed through the paperwork to make my arrival official.

"Of course," the lieutenant said with a sneer of

insincerity. "It's a waste of resources to uncover the mud huts of ancient savages. They probably ate their young like the beasts of the forests. Best to leave the past buried."

Yesterday, we'd uncovered a sacrificial altar in the center of the town square. Every culture practiced sacrifice, whether it was animal, fasting, or even human. The practice of surrendering what was held dear continued today when a father went without for his child, a wife put her husband's needs before her own, or a junior executive let go of pride to grasp onto a higher ladder rung toward success. At its core, sacrifice was giving up what one held dear for the greater good. In a way, I supposed the government's attempt to hide this find to protect the current cultural identity was a sacrifice. Still, it didn't make it right.

"The IAC sent me to ground truth the site and authenticate the findings, in accordance with the International Antiquities Agreement. They believe this find has great historical significance that could benefit all mankind."

The lieutenant raised that eyebrow again as though he didn't believe me. Damn, he was smarter than I'd thought. But I didn't have the time or inclination to offer him any credit when his men were stealing credit from another culture from the dig site.

"My country does not need an agreement to dig in our own backyard," he said.

"No, but you will need help in recovering anything that might be looted and taken to another country. I think the location of the site has been leaked online."

I was finally getting to the reason I'd raced from the satellite phone, where I'd been checking email in my tent, to the dig site. I hadn't been online since getting here. When I'd logged on twenty minutes ago, there'd been an alert of increased activity on the darknet site that had led me here.

"Nonsense," the lieutenant drawled. "And even if the location got out, my men are covering the entire area."

"But there's a lot of ground to cover," I insisted. "Perhaps if you don't stretch your men so thin, and instead move them closer to the site itself—"

"Ms. Rivers, I know Americans let their women have a voice, but you are in my country, in the middle of a jungle, speaking to a ranking officer of the military. Giving orders might not be the best use of your voice."

I was good at affecting an American accent, but I

wasn't American. And, yes, that was what I chose to focus on instead of his misogynistic comments. I had been around him too many days to give this new spin on his age-old record any more play. There were more important things at stake.

"The only place where any of this junk is going is a government vault," he said, looking around with disgust.

"You mean a vault with the National Antiquities Coalition of Honduras?" I asked, injecting a note of sweetness into my voice.

I'd been around too many men and women like him—people more interested in protecting their interests than advancing humanity—to let this slide. The Honduran government had no intention of letting this information get out until they could figure out how to make it play to their benefit. And when they figured it out, the truth of this lost civilization would be doctored and diluted, conquered and colonized, until it fit with the national identity currently in place.

To the victor goes the spoils, or so the saying went. Unfortunately for the government, I had every intention of being the victor today.

"Once our experts authenticate the ... artifacts, we will decide what to share outside of our borders," the lieutenant said, a condescending note in his voice. "Don't worry that pretty little head of yours about raiders. You are well protected here."

He was wrong. I had gotten in.

His words were a threat, despite his attempt to "placate" me. I knew I should show fear—my lack thereof would only excite him, push him to challenge me more. But I was too tired and grumpy about my soiled clothing to pretend I was cowed.

"Whatever," I finally said with a shrug. "Maybe I'm wrong." I knew I wasn't.

Lieutenant Alvarenga nodded his head sagely. "If you are concerned for your safety, you can always stop by my tent after dark."

"Tempting." My tone was sardonic, but the glint in his eyes told me he didn't catch the scorn. If I was going to crawl around in the dirt, I at least wanted to dig up something worth my trouble.

I turned on my heel and headed back to my tent, feeling his eyes on my ass. That was fine. It was the last he'd see of it.

CHAPTER TWO

The night was loud. Mammals, reptiles, and insects yawned themselves awake and then began their rituals. Crickets rubbed their thighs together to announce their availability. Birds flapped their wings as they sang night songs. Howler monkeys justified their names and bellowed to one another across the branches.

Down below the night's activity, an anteater crossed my path, stopped, and turned to stare at me where I hid in a crouch. He licked at the mud on my boots but, finding no ants, kept going. He wasn't my only visitor. The animals of this lush forest hadn't seen humans in a millennium. They'd forgotten how to be afraid.

I climbed up the tree trunk to avoid the further attention of the ground dwellers and to get a better vantage point. A sloth swung by and crawled over to the branch next to me. Its arms and legs held on to the branch, and it looked at me upside down. We eyed each other for a few moments. I lost the staring contest and giggled at the serious expression on its smooshed face.

The snick of a branch cracking in the distance brought my attention back to the matter at hand. Turning my head, I started at the sight of two of the lieutenant's soldiers. I recognized them from camp. Apparently, the lieutenant had heeded my warning. Unfortunately for him, it was too late.

The soldiers kept their eyes on the horizon, their gazes fixed on where the sun had set. Something told me to look up toward the new moon. I saw the raiders then. Heart pounding, I counted three of them moving through the treetops above me.

Dammit.

I'd known they were coming, but I'd hoped it wouldn't be so soon. They moved through the rainforest canopy like wraiths, silent enough that any sounds they made blended with the noises of the other animals flitting from branch to branch. If not for my gut instinct, I never would have noticed them.

Tensing my body, I kept as quiet and still as I could and studied them. Two of the raiders were locals. I could tell by the way they moved lithely through the dark. The third, the leader, was a foreigner. He was likely a young man studied in the new-age art of parkour. But tree branches were not like rooftops or concrete half-pipes, and he lagged. It wasn't long before he slipped. The branch beneath him, too slight to hold his weight, cracked.

I watched with bated breath as the man grabbed hold of the tree trunk. From yards away, I saw his fingers turn pale as they held fast. His lips moved rapidly, probably praying to whatever god he believed in that nobody would see him. Or, if he was smart, that he wouldn't fall.

The branch snapped. The break was clean. The thick piece of bark turned over, top to bottom, on its way down. Its young leaves were stripped of twigs as the branch fell.

But it was the only thing that fell. The man had managed to wrap his legs around another branch and was now holding on to the tree trunk with his fingernails and feet crossed at the ankles. Much like my sloth companion.

The branch hit the ground with a heavy thud, and one of the soldiers was instantly alerted. He looked left and right. Thankfully for the parkourist, the soldier didn't look up.

The soldier peered around for another minute but then turned and marched away. His thunderous steps cleared the animals from his path, making way for the thieves in the night. The tree climbers pulled out anaconda-thick ropes and began quietly rappelling their way to the ground. When they hit the terrain floor, they crept toward the dig site.

I rose from my crouch in the trees, bidding farewell to the staring sloth before swan-diving straight off the branch. The wind whistled past my ears as I tucked my body into a double flip, then landed soundlessly with sure feet on the damp rainforest floor. Not that my silent landing did me any good.

Straightening, I found myself face to face with one of the soldiers. My heart jumped into my throat. His eyes immediately went wide with terror. The sweat that broke out on his temples had nothing to do with the ever-present humidity.

"*El espíritu*," he whispered, stumbling backward. "*El espíritu!*"

His frightened shout echoed through the trees,

and I sighed. My cover was blown. I'd traded in my jeans and linen blouse for a dark tunic that covered my legs and torso. The head covering that masked my face did a decent job of hiding my identity. With the ornamental design on the strap of the bush sword hanging over my shoulder, I supposed I did look like a vengeful Mayan goddess.

The second soldier came running into the clearing, gun already drawn. He stopped short at the sight of me. In the near distance, the raider and his cronies paused to watch the commotion.

"I wouldn't do that—" I began as the soldier raised his shaking gun at me, but he didn't listen.

He squeezed off two shots in succession, one flying wide, the other winging straight for me despite his terrible aim. I deflected that one easily with my blade, but his third shot was steadier. It hit the leather strap of my sword case; the strap snapped in two, and my bag fell to the ground.

Anger ripped through me, and I sucked in a deep breath as I brushed the residual metal scraps off my top. Dirt, I could get out. But the torn fabric where the bullet hole had bounced off my skin was another matter. The soldier tried to squeeze off another shot, but I closed the distance in less than a second. My fingers dug into his neck as I picked him up off the ground.

Gritting my teeth, I slammed him against the tree trunk. His head knocked against the bark with a satisfying thunk, and his eyes rolled back into his head as he immediately passed out. Curling my lip, I released him. His body slumped to the ground like a broken doll, gun hanging uselessly at his side.

But at least he'd live.

I turned toward the second soldier, but he was already gone, crashing through the bushes as he sprinted away. Two of the raiders were right behind him, flitting through the trees as if their lives depended on it. But the parkourist had gone ahead while I'd been distracted. Through the clearing, I watched him race off into the ruins.

I sighed and headed off in his direction at no great rush. Even though we were out in the open, there was only one way in and out of the area, and he was running straight into the out door. I was never one to sneer during a horror movie when the villain or the monster strolled after the distressed, erratically running damsel or clumsy dumb dude. They always ran into the trap.

But then, I heard a crash and the splintering sound of a thousand years' worth of knowledge being smashed. The raider, who'd tripped over a carefully plotted, roped-off area of the dig, was straightening from his face-plant.

Seriously? I'd encountered rhinoceroses more graceful than this guy. My heart turned to stone as I zeroed in on the remains of a vase shattered in the dirt. I took off after him, my powerful legs eating up the ground much faster than any human runner could manage. Hell, I'd even outrun cheetahs once. I was on him before he took his next breath.

With one hand, I grabbed him, then tossed him into an unmarked section of the grass. He landed with an even louder thud than the branch he'd snapped. By the time his eyes blinked open, my foot was pressed into his chest.

"Do you have any idea of the value of what you just destroyed?" I demanded.

He sputtered, his eyes bugging out, and I knew he was seeing the same vengeful spirit the others had.

"The knowledge we would have gained from that single unbroken piece could have filled an entire volume. *Would have filled,*" I added with a snarl, "if you hadn't just destroyed it with your clumsy footwork."

I eased up on his throat a bit so he could whine

and beg. But he only stared up at me in muted confusion. I began to snap at him again, but I suddenly realized I had spoken to him in my native tongue, which was older than English or Spanish. Older than Latin, Hebrew, or any other language still spoken today.

"W-what are you?" he stammered.

The way his lower lip trembled made him look like a damn kid. Unfortunately for him, my sympathy meter was low. I felt more for the broken vase than I did for this petulant child.

"A-are you really a vengeful spirit?" He covered his face with trembling hands. "Oh, God."

The stench of urine laced the air, and I curled my lip at him.

He pulled his hands away from his face. "This is your tomb, isn't it? And now you're going to curse me for trying to steal your treasures!"

"Sure," I said dryly, easing back a little. "We can go with that."

I took a moment to study the man-child who'd somehow grown enough balls to try to rob this dig site. He couldn't have been more than twenty-five. Probably watched *Indiana Jones* as a kid, played *Assassin's Creed* as a teen. He was likely an adrenaline junkie looking to make a quick buck.

An idea popped into my head, and my lips curved into a wicked smile. I could make use of this guy. "The curse is upon you," I said, filling my voice with Spanish flair even though the ancient people who lived here a millennium ago had never met a Spaniard. "If you want to break the curse and curry my favor, you'll do as I wish ... or your family will perish."

"Yes," he immediately agreed, his voice filled with a combination of fear and eagerness. "I understand."

I stepped back and let him up. He rose on wobbly legs. His hands went to cover the wet spot of his cargo pants.

"My people have long been hidden," I intoned in a grave, ancient voice. "It is past time for the world to know about us. You shall be the one to tell them. Follow me."

I turned on my heel without another word. He scrambled after me like an eager puppy, but I could tell he was being careful not to crush any more artifacts.

I led him further into the tomb, to the artifact that had first caught my eye when I came here. It was a clay tablet with writings etched into it that predated the Mayan script. I'd already started translating the tablet. It told a different story than the Maya and their descendants told.

According to the writings, these two cultures had met. The Maya had learned much from this older, more learned culture. I knew that if I left the tablet here the Honduran government would steal it away and bury it so their dirty secret wouldn't get out. But I couldn't let them do that. This tablet was bigger than their need for tourism. On it were clues as to why this civilization fell. It was likely because the people turned on their gods, which was a common reason.

Gently, I plucked the tablet from its perch. After wrapping it in a protective cloth, I handed it to my delivery boy along with a business card.

"Take my story to this address," I said. "And handle it with care."

The raider took the tablet and cradled it in his arms. He stuffed the business card into his pocket. If he wondered how a millennia-old goddess happened to be in possession of a business card with a Washington, D.C. address, he didn't mention it.

Looking him squarely in the eye, I warned, "If you betray me, I will find you."

I took a step forward, and he gulped when I patted his cheek.

"Be careful," I said softly. "The next time you plan to raid a tomb, the god you find inside may not be as kind."

Nodding, he took off like a rocket. As I watched him sprint out of the tomb, I prayed he was better at escaping than he was at breaking and entering.

CHAPTER THREE

"When most people think of archaeology, they think of fossils and mummies. They picture huge reptiles buried beneath the ground. They imagine great rulers hidden in triangular castles in the sand. As archaeologists, what we do is bigger than that."

I stood in front of a crowd of fifty professors, professionals, and students in the theater of the National Museum of the American Indian at the Smithsonian Institution in Washington, D.C. Believe it or not, fifty was a stadium-sized crowd in my field. The numerous prescription lenses in the crowd reflected off the bright fluorescent lights. Pencils belonging to the older crowd worked furiously over notepads. The nimble fingers of the younger ones flew over keyboards and handheld devices to capture my jewels of knowledge.

"We're not just uncovering physical relics of the past, we are uncovering ideas. We think we are innovative, only to see that it has been done before."

A raised platform stood next to my lectern. I pulled the sheet covering it to reveal the tablet the parkourist had hand-delivered to one of my colleagues at the Smithsonian. The young man had managed to deliver it without a nick or even a raised flag from customs.

The Honduran government hadn't been happy, but I had warned Lieutenant Alvarenga about the raiders. Though he was no longer a lieutenant. Letting out the inarguable facts of this older culture had cost him his rank. Now the entire world knew a civilization predated the Maya. The stories of these lost people would finally be told.

"History books are written by the victors," I continued. "But sometimes, those winners lie. It's important to unearth not only a pharaoh, but also the pharaoh's servant. When you go out there and dig, search for the marginalized, the minorities, and the underrepresented. Give them a voice. Their stories matter. All tales must be told, even the ugly ones—especially the ugly ones."

The applause from the smattering of audience members might as well have been the boom of a rock concert. I wasn't often recognized for the work I did; I preferred the shadows and the cover of night to run my crusades of discoveries of the dead. But this long-dead story had to be told, and I was the only living one who could tell it.

I stepped off the platform and fielded a few questions, declining selfies with excuses ranging from needing to keep my identity quiet so I could participate in secret digs—true—to photokeratitis—not true, but fun to say.

A notification on my phone got me out of a one-sided debate with a tall man in a tweed suit. I could tell by his incessant inhaling and rubbing at the back of his neck that he was working up the courage to ask for my number. I was amusing myself trying to decide if he was going to ask me out for drinks or to coauthor a paper with him. I couldn't tell.

Either way, the answer would've been no. I didn't want the notoriety that came with signing my name to published documents. And the reason I wasn't interested in drinks with him was ringing my phone right now.

I turned my back, hoping the junior professor would get the message and stop trying to further build up his courage. When he kept hovering patiently, I moved closer to the window and then out of the building entirely.

The cell reception inside the museum wasn't poor. I had full bars, but the text message still took its time loading onto the screen. I stepped outside into the cool afternoon air and waited, refreshing my phone every other second.

Finally, the picture came through. It was fuzzy and hazy, but I made out my own face in the painting. There was a rainbow of reds from the lightest of pinks to the darkest of fuchsias. At the center of the canvas was a nude woman reclining with her arms thrown above her head. Her bare thighs were squeezed together, and her toes were curled as though she'd been assaulted with more pleasure than she could handle. Her lips were parted in a sated grin. She had one eye closed and the other open with a sparkle at its center. He'd painted me just like I'd been the last time he'd seen me.

Below the picture was a text message bubble. It read, *This is how I spent my Manboobs.*

I snorted and hit reply. *I take it your Monday is going well? Love the fuckweasel.*

I hadn't typed *fuckweasel* on my end, but when

the "delivered" notification popped up below the text bubble on my phone, I knew the *autocucumber* had struck again.

Autocorrect was a constant bane in our relationship. No matter how many times either of us proofed our words, the text messages were a little wrong and often dirtier than we'd intended. Sexting was a comedy of errors with his *pumas* and my *china* doing all manner of naughty things.

I waited patiently for the reply. It came a full two minutes later.

God donut, fuchsia is beautiful against your skin.

He said that about every color. My lover, Zane, had painted me in every color of the spectrum. I aimed my thumb to prepare for another text when my phone screen went dark.

I hit the home button and got no response. Then I held the power button at the top of the device. Still not a flicker.

I cursed under my breath, preparing to toss the device down the steps. But I didn't. I knew the malfunction wasn't my phone's fault. I tried not to take it too personally. I'd be seeing him later tonight, after all.

I pocketed the phone. It would turn back on when it was ready. By then, Zane would be lost in whatever piece of art he was working on. Once he got in the zone, he wouldn't pay attention to anything but the creation at his fingertips.

I knew that firsthand. The details of that nude portrait of me were intricate and meticulous—down to the slight freckling on my high cheekbones. Thankfully, he'd pleasured me into an oblivion before he'd picked up his paints to capture the aftermath. He hadn't come to bed until the work of art was finished. Zane was nothing if not dedicated to his work.

"Excuse me, Dr. Rivers?"

My hand brushed the blade strapped to my upper thigh. The weapon was tucked in a compartment sewn into the pocket of my pantsuit. My movement was an automatic response whenever anyone came up behind me. I'd been too distracted by Zane to notice the woman's approach.

I knew it was a woman. Her accent was African. The consonants came off her tongue clipped and harsh like she was South African. But she added a softening to the end of my name, lengthening the vowel sound as though she had leisure time at her hands and the freedom to spend it. An Afrikaner, maybe?

"You *are* Dr. Nia Rivers, antiquities expert?"

The question was a challenge. I turned to see Charlize Theron's younger, prettier sister. Her pale skin was deeply tanned; it was a healthy tan that came from the sun and not a tanning bed. Her blonde hair was knotted low at the back of her swan's neck. The woman's cool blue gaze raked over me in assessment. Mine did the same in the way of two lionesses on a savanna, two princesses eyeing the crown, two cheerleaders angling for the top of the pyramid.

"You're a hard woman to track down," she said.

No, I was an impossible woman to track down. My skills were sought after, but I gave clients a wide window of when I might arrive on a site, never a firm date. My preference was to simply pop up without notice like I'd done in Honduras. I didn't like people knowing my daily itinerary.

My hand brushed the hidden blade on my thigh again. The woman's eyes flicked down to my motion. Her penciled brows arched, but she kept her hands on her bag strap. My eyes caught the bag—vintage Gucci. Nice.

Her eyes went to my boots. They were Stuart Weitzman. Hers were Kenneth Cole. Stylish boots with good soles and protective leather. Her skirt was designer—Stella McCartney. My pants were Prada. Our gazes met back at the center.

"I'm Loren Van Alst, Import/Export specialist."

I quirked a brow, shifting my assessment. Again, her eyes flicked almost imperceptibly. Ms. Van Alst continued as though she hadn't caught my disapproval. Import/Export was synonymous with tomb raider as far as I was concerned.

But Loren smiled confidently at me, like she had a secret. She reached into her designer bag and pulled out an 8x10 photo. The sun reflected on the white back of the photo paper as she held the image close to her chest.

"I could use your expertise with authenticating an artifact."

I decided to bite. "What kind of artifact?"

Her blue eyes danced. She thought she had me. "You've heard of dragon bones?"

I had. Dragon bones were an ancient record-keeping method before paper made its way through Asia. Past events of note and future predictions for the noble class were etched on turtle shells and ox scapula.

"I found one." Loren tapped her manicured fingernail on the back of the photograph.

"I thought you said you were in Import/Export," I said.

"I am." She smiled. "I specialize in ancient artifacts."

"You can always call up the IAC," I said. "They can hook you up with an authenticator. I'm due out of the country tomorrow."

I was able to reschedule my spa trip, and my plane was leaving in the morning. Nothing short of the Holy Grail would get me to miss my date with manufactured mud, a man-made sauna, and artificial indoor lights. And I knew for a fact that the Grail was locked under sword and key.

I turned from Ms. Van Alst and began to head down the steps.

"I doubt anyone else from the IAC could read this," she called out. "I've never seen writing like this. The script predates any ancient Chinese writing on record. It looks to be older than the Shang Dynasty. Languages are your specialty."

I slowed my pace as I reached the last step. Languages *were* my specialty. Like a stamp or baseball card collector, I collected languages. I knew all of them ever written or spoken.

My ears perked up like a dog smelling a meaty bone. I didn't like being baited or manipulated into doing anything. And this woman clearly knew my weak spots.

Before I turned back around, I constructed a bland mask over my face. It would've been easier if I'd had a facial in the last week. I had meant to look Loren Van Alst in the eye when I spun around. Unfortunately, I miscalculated.

When I turned, Ms. Van Alst had come down a couple of steps so that her chest was directly in my sight line. She'd already turned the photographic paper my way. My gaze caught on her trimmed nail and the characters it pointed to in the photograph.

I didn't hear anything else she said. My heart raced, urging me to step closer to the image. My brain fogged, trying to reach out through the haze. My fingers ached from the memory of carving characters into bone.

This dragon bone was authentic. I knew it to be true like I knew my own name, because I was looking at my name on the carving of the bone in the picture. That was my signature on the two-thousand-year-old artifact. I had written that message.

CHAPTER FOUR

I watched as Loren swirled her glass of expensive wine. We sat in the courtyard bar of the American Art Museum. The bar was indoors but the windows were wall to wall, allowing patrons to see outside and onto the lawn of the Smithsonian. Workers milled about, scarfing down paper-bag lunches and trying to catch a small dose of vitamin D before they had to go back into the windowless cubicles. I'd never sat in a cubicle a day in my life. I doubt I could stand the confinement. I was feeling trapped enough by my companion as she stood there holding the information hostage.

Loren had long since put the photograph back in her vintage bag. It was no matter. I'd committed the markings to memory. Although my short-term memory was photographic, it was the longer-term ones that had the tendency to fade—like photographic paper. I'd need to transcribe the markings I'd seen onto paper to translate all the words. I could only make out a few of the meanings, and what little I understood didn't make sense.

"It's uncanny," Loren said. "The woman in that painting..."

I turned and looked through the large picture windows into the gallery. The portrait Loren indicated was of a dark-haired woman in an eighteenth-century ball gown sitting alone on a courting bench. The secret smile on her lips told the viewers she didn't expect to be sitting alone for long.

And I hadn't sat alone for long. Zane had joined me as soon as he'd painted the last stroke. But we hadn't stayed on the bench. The gown hadn't stayed on my body either.

"She could be your younger sister," Loren mused.

I inhaled slowly through gritted teeth. She didn't know she was insulting my age. I looked exactly the same as I had two hundred years ago.

"An ancient relative, maybe?" she asked, eyes still locked on Zane's painting. "What *is* your cultural heritage?"

I didn't know. I was a mix of everything. Brown skin that could be Asian or Spanish or African. Angular features that could be Indian or Egyptian or Irish. I had no idea where I came from or who I belonged to. That memory had faded a few millennia ago.

I turned from the painting as a man in a museum service uniform passed by the work of art that depicted me in another time period and focused my attention on the woman in front of me.

"So, Ms. Van Alst." I paused, waiting to see if she corrected the title. Like married women, women with doctorates always corrected their salutation. Loren didn't. In fact, she smiled at me like she knew exactly what I was doing. "Where did you study?"

"I believe you Americans call it the *School of Hard Knocks*. My dad had the degrees. I tagged along on his expeditions and learned on the job."

"Van Alst?" A memory tugged at the corner of my mind. It wasn't a glowing one. The Dr. Van Alst I was remembering had been cast aside in disgrace.

"Yep, that Van Alst." Loren said it with her head held high, waiting for a challenge.

Dr. Van Alst had been renowned for his work ten years ago. But a forged artifact had brought it all crumbling down. That forged artifact had been a dragon bone.

The man had claimed the bone was from the Xia people of Asia. Most historians believe the Xia were a small tribe in ancient China that had thrived for a brief period before the more well-known Shang Dynasty. No one conceded the Xia qualified as a dynasty.

The dragon bone Dr. Van Alst found proclaimed the tribe to have been led by a queen. That hadn't helped his case. There was no record of a female ruler in China. Soon after that, the bone was declared a fraud carved on a fossil stolen from a modern-day museum. Van Alst copped to the forgery, but he swore the markings he'd drawn were real and that he'd copied them from the real bone, which he said the modern-day Xia wouldn't allow him to take. To this day, no one had ever found the site.

It looked like the younger Van Alst was on this mission for redemption and not necessarily to raid the Chinese of their ancient riches. Dammit, I was a sucker for a good underdog story. I turned away from Loren's steely shoulders and stiff upper lip. Once again, my eye caught the museum worker.

The man was unscrewing a painting beside the

one of me from the wall. On the floor was a frame with "Out for Cleaning" written on it. No alarm sounded, but a bell rang in my head. It was curious because I happened to know that all restoration work was done after closing hours.

"Aren't you going to ask?" Loren said, snapping my attention back to her.

"If the bone is authentic?" I shook my head. I knew it was. Not only because of my signature and what I had already translated, but because I knew this woman wasn't stupid. If she had the balls to go after the artifact that had disgraced her father, she'd make damn sure it was the real deal.

"Where exactly did you find the bone?" I sipped my pomegranate martini and watched the worker struggle with the bolt on the painting. He was wrenching the bolt to the right. Apparently, he didn't know the old adage of *lefty-loosey, righty-tighty*.

"The Gongyi province in southern China," she said.

Damn, that was deep in the heart of the country —nowhere near a proper city. I grimaced, turning back to Loren. She'd missed the look on my face. Her attention was also on the worker. She spoke to me as we watched him struggle with the bolt.

"I noticed you haven't done work in China in the

last five years that you've been working with the IAC."

She was wrong. I hadn't done work in China since before the IAC was founded.

"How do you know so much about me to begin with?" I asked. "My work with the IAC isn't exactly publicized."

"I'm good at puzzles, and I see your pattern," she said, catching my gaze. "Lost civilization, government lockdown, and there you are. You're easy to find if you know where to look. I knew you were in Honduras. When I saw that artifact pop up on the—" She coughed into her hand to cover the word she nearly let slip. Then she put her fist to her chest, as though to excuse herself, and began again. "When I saw it pop up on the Smithsonian registry, I figured you were behind it and decided to head here."

I knew her fake cough was to catch herself from outing her knowledge of the darknet site for tomb raiders. But it was the fact that she saw a pattern in my movements that made me most uncomfortable. If she could find me, that meant other people could. Luckily, I was getting out of here in the morning.

"So..." Loren said. "You're in? You'll come to

China, ground truth the site, authenticate the artifact, and help me translate the bones?"

I chuckled. She had balls, this one. That was four things she'd asked me for. The problem was I couldn't do the first item on her list.

"I went ahead and procured you a first-class ticket to Beijing." Loren reached into her bag and pulled out an airline ticket.

"I'm not flying to Beijing." I put down my empty glass.

"Why not? They've done some serious upgrades to the terminal in the last year. They even have a spa."

"Really?" My ears perked up. "Wait, no. I'm not going to China."

I hadn't been to China since before the invention of air travel. Probably hadn't been back to China since I wrote on that turtle shell. It was a partial message. It looked like the end of a warning about ghosts in the forests and a queen. I needed the rest of the bones to decipher the entire message.

"Listen," I said. "I believe that bone is authentic. And I will help you decipher whatever you find. Just bring the other bones to me when you're done with the excavation."

"Well, that sounds like a swell plan." Loren

pressed her lips into a thin smile. "Only I can't get back onto the site. A developer has leased the land from the local government and made it off limits. Maybe you've heard of him? Tresor Mohandis."

I pinched the stem of my empty wineglass at the sound of that name, hurriedly letting it go before I broke the glass with the slight pressure from my thumb.

"Yeah, I thought that would get your attention." Loren's thin grin spread triumphantly. "From what I can tell, you've successfully stopped him from building on three sites in the last five years by helping to get the land marked protected and historical."

I'd fouled his plans more than five times, and for a much longer time than I cared to remember. If my life were a comic book, Tres Mohandis would be my arch enemy. Our battles for territory across the globe and over the centuries were epic.

"Through the government, Mohandis has put an injunction on the land," Loren continued. "So no more excavation or even pleasure hiking. I don't have the credentials to prove what I found so the site could be marked historical. No one else will bother to move against him because he's lining their pockets with money. Plus, the locals..."

She took a deep breath, turning away from my inquisitive gaze.

"Let's just say they didn't take kindly to my being on their sacred land. Meanwhile, I think there's more than just bones there. I think it's a lost civilization. It might be the home of the ancient Xia. I think there are more artifacts there to prove they were a dynasty and not just a series of tribes."

This woman was very good. She knew dead languages were my catnip and that Tres Mohandis was my Achilles' heel. Now she went for the kill by implying a potential lost civilization.

"Where's the bone now?" I asked.

"Where I found it," she said, still not meeting my eyes. "I didn't have time to properly excavate and move it before the locals found me and the Mohandis security barred me from the land."

That shocked me. For a raider, she had a healthy respect for the artifact. I'd seen too many smash-and-grab jobs by other raiders over the years, rendering artifacts nothing more than dust.

"Mohandis had you and your team physically removed from the land?"

"It wasn't Mohandis," she said. "It was some overzealous local men who were trying to protect their heritage from nasty foreigners. And I was there by myself."

I shook my head at the admission. "A tomb raider through and through."

"Right, I'm labeled a raider because I don't have a team and degrees? The work I do is just as important as what you do."

"No, the difference is I share the knowledge, not sell it to the highest bidder."

"Fine," Loren said. "So, I'm smarter than you because I get compensated for my work."

"Knowledge lasts longer than riches, trust me."

"Maybe." Loren sat back and crossed her arms over her chest. "But people will choose money in the present over notoriety in the future every day. And Mohandis Enterprises knows how to capitalize off that. He's going to build on that site in a couple of weeks without looking back at yesterday. Then the truth of my father's work will be forever lost, and so will the voices, lives, and history of those ancient people."

I swore that bastard purposely sought out ancient lands to build his modern, metallic, homogenous behemoths.

"Is it just me or is that guy about to steal that painting?" Loren asked.

I turned my attention back to the service worker. I had been thinking the same thing. "It's not a hard thing to do. The Smithsonian only cares what you bring in the doors. They're not as good at monitoring what you take out."

The metal detectors hadn't gone off at the blade on my hip. It was made of jade, not steel. Most items in this museum, like the parchment that painting was on, weren't metal. So the detectors brooked no argument if they left without their metal encasements.

"Tell me about it," Loren said, sipping the last of her wine. "Did you hear about what happened to the snuff box they had from Catherine the Great?"

"Don't remind me," I moaned.

Someone had snuck out with the priceless artifact that the Russian queen had given to her lover Count Orlov. And that time, the alarm bells had rung in the museum. But the treasure was lost by the time they tracked it down. The diamonds had been removed and sold, and the gold melted down.

The worker had finally figured out his right from his left and was working on the last bolt.

"Did you hear the one about the mail clerk who walked out with ten, ancient books from the Natural History Museum?" I asked.

Loren hmphed. "They might as well leave the doors of that museum open; it's so easy to walk out with anything."

Jerking my head toward her, I didn't miss the wince, as though she'd said too much. A turtle shell had gone missing from the Natural History Museum about the time her father came out with his fake dragon bone.

"So, should we do something?" Loren asked.

"We shouldn't have to." I pushed away my empty martini glass. "Supposedly, security has improved."

The painting sprang free from the wall. The man stumbled back as the weight of the frame came into his arms. Loren and I gasped as the priceless work of art shuffled about in his arms only feet away from the hard floor.

The man regained his footing. His gaze went up to the security guard standing at the threshold that led from the courtyard bar to the interior of the museum. The security guard rolled his eyes in annoyance, but he made no move to stop him.

So, it was an inside job.

The thief put the painting on the floor and raised the "Out for Cleaning" sign to take its place. I rose from my seat in disbelief that the idiot would set a one-of-a-kind piece directly on the damn ground.

"Oh, no, he didn't," Loren hissed. She reached into her bag and pulled out a baton. Giving it a hard shake, she turned it into a cane like the kind I'd trained with in dojos. This was about to get ugly.

Loren strapped her vintage bag over her shoulder and headed into the museum. I moved into gear to catch up. We passed the security guard, who eyed us nervously.

"I think you misplaced something," Loren said as she approached the thief. She placed herself between the thief and the painting.

"Oh, don't worry your pretty little head," he said. "I've got it."

The man went to reach for the painting, but the whack from Loren's cane stopped him. With my pinky finger, I caught the heavy weight of the wobbling painting and stopped it from teetering to the ground. No one saw my interference. Everyone's eyes were on Loren and the service worker.

"No, you didn't misplace the painting," she said. "I think you misplaced your worker ID card. Can you pull it out for me?"

The man cradled his injured hand and glared.

"What's going on here?" the security guard said as he came over.

"I'm glad you're here," Loren said. "Do you recognize this man?"

The security guard gulped. It was a trick question. If he admitted he did recognize him, it would be clear he was in on the theft. If he didn't recognize him, then he was showing he hadn't been doing his job.

"Security," Loren shouted. "And I mean real security this time."

Everyone in the hall stopped to witness the commotion. The thief had a look of panic in his eyes. He turned to run, but his feet met with the blunt end of Loren's cane and he tripped. She pulled a set of plastic handcuffs out of her bag and bound him.

"What else do you have in that bag?" I queried.

She winked at me as she finished binding the thief. Then her head turned like a bloodhound scenting prey. The security guard had reached for the painting. Loren lunged, like I'd seen fencers do. With her cane as an extension of her arm, she struck the guard's hands before he could touch the painting.

"If you're going to steal," she said, "at least have respect for the thing you're stealing. Putting a priceless painting on the floor? Didn't your parents teach you manners?"

More security came into the fray. "What's going on?" one of them shouted.

"They were going to steal the painting," someone from the crowd shouted.

"And that woman stopped them," another patron added.

The crowd engulfed Loren in an excited hum, swallowing her whole as the other guards took care of the traitor and his accomplice.

I edged myself to the exit, but not before Loren caught my gaze. When I raised my hand in a farewell salute, she reached into her bag, pulled out the airline ticket, and waved the slip of paper at me. I ducked out the door into the courtyard, unsure which way to go. So, I just walked.

CHAPTER FIVE

There were rumors that several cell towers in Washington, D.C. were dummy towers. I didn't know if it was true, but it made sense with all the embassies of countries that liked to spy on one another lined up in nice rows on one street. The name of the street was even called Embassy Row.

That evening, I made my way down to 12th Street. With laptop in hand, I climbed to the top of the Federal Communications Building. I figured the FCC would be the last place to lose a connection and the strongest place to make one. It was date night, and I wasn't taking any chances.

I watched the sun set in the capital. It was one of the prettiest sight lines in the nation. That was because of the regulations about building heights. Most believed that there was a law that restricted the heights of buildings to less than 130 feet because no structure could rise higher than the Capitol. But that was a myth. It had more to do with the width of the narrow streets relative to the heights of the buildings. The upside of the rule was that the skyline was actually visible.

Down below, trees intermingled with stone and steel. Up above, the horizon was an ombre of blues. The white smoke of chimneys reached into the pale of periwinkle where the skyline began. As the sun slipped deeper into the cover of night, a blanket of azure spread across the sky.

It was the type of view Zane would feel compelled to immortalize in his art. I arranged myself in front of the laptop camera so the skyline was my backdrop. Twenty minutes later, the ringtone of an incoming video call sounded.

Zane's face filled the screen. His dark hair fell in front of his dark eyes. His lashes were so thick that he always appeared to be squinting. One corner of his mouth was parked upward in a perpetual smile. Even when he was annoyed with me, which was surprisingly often, he looked as though he was amused with my antics.

He ran a hand through his damp hair as he settled his lithe body in front of his computer camera. He was shirtless. I could make out beads of moisture on his defined chest. He'd come from the shower, but his hand still had streaks of paint and hardened clay at his fingertips and knuckles.

"There is my goddess, my muse. Amen, *mon coeur*." His hand reached out to the screen to trace what he saw on his side of the connection. "*Mon dieu*, I always forget how perfect your cheekbones are."

He reached for something off screen. It was a pencil without an eraser and a sketchpad. I knew better than to stop him. But it had been weeks since I'd seen his face or heard his voice. I wanted his attention on the live me and not the one he was about to capture on parchment.

"Zane."

"*Oui, ma petite nova.*"

I listened to the pencil scratching the parchment. It was funny how one sense could spark the memories of another. The sound of the lead brought me to a memory of the first time we met. It was in Florence, Italy, in the fifteenth century where he'd been employed as a mentor teaching sculpture and painting to artists.

He'd stopped mid-speech, turning away from

his students, his gaze locked on my form as I came near. His immobility had not been because he'd recognized his own kind. Well, that had caught his attention. It was the effect we Immortals had on one another. But then his gaze found and held mine.

When he'd taken a step toward me, my hand reached for the daggers beneath my skirts, assuming I would encounter a threat. He caught my hand movements and the glint at my thigh and grinned. The cold steel was clearly visible in my hand, but he kept walking toward me with that confident swagger and devil-may-care grin.

I didn't loosen my grip, nor did I take my eyes off him. I didn't move as he came to stand before me with only a paintbrush in his hand to defend himself.

He told me my cheekbones were perfection and asked if I would pose for him. After repeating his request twice in my head, I barked out a laugh and declined. He smiled, completely unfazed, and watched me as I walked away.

It wasn't the last time I saw him. He managed to pop up wherever I happened to be every couple of years, like he could predict my movements. For the next hundred years, he continued to pursue me across two continents. Until I finally held still long enough for him to paint me.

I was content to hold still for him now, like I always did. Time stopped when I was with Zane, which was funny. Time didn't move normally for either of us.

We'd been on this earth for thousands of years. Exactly how many thousands? Neither of us were sure. None of the Immortals knew for certain how long we'd been here. None of us could remember exactly how we'd gotten here. Whether we were human or something else entirely.

We all didn't talk to each other much. We were impervious to disease, physical assault, and time. Our only weakness was each other. We jokingly called it an allergy.

For some reason that none of us knew, we began to weaken when we were in each other's presence for too long. It might start with a tickle in the throat. A week later, the fatigue would settle in and we wouldn't heal as quickly if injured. After a month or two, the door to our impenetrable immune system would open. Once it did, any manner of disease, malady, and injury could befall us. In a sense, we made each other human.

So, of course, I went and fell in love with one of

my own kind—a man I could only see for a small amount of time or suffer contraindications. Zane literally made my heart skip beats. He made my knees weak. I went stupid whenever I saw his face or heard his voice.

I watched as he continued his sketching in the present. He'd drawn my form countless times over the last half millennium, but he never seemed to tire. And it wasn't only me that he depicted in his artwork.

Zane had been drawing, painting, and sculpting for as long as he could remember. But he rarely got the opportunity to take credit for his work. His technique evolved. His name changed. But his face didn't. He was careful how often he went out in public, especially these days when information from across the globe was at everyone's fingertips with the touch of a button.

In the past, he'd contented himself with teaching his techniques so that the influence of his artwork could be shared. When I'd met him in Florence all those centuries ago, he'd been teaching a twelve-year-old boy named Michelangelo the art of fresco, which was painting on plaster with watercolors. It was a technique Zane had perfected in Egypt. But it wasn't until his pupil grew up and painted on the ceiling of a church that the practice took on a new life.

Zane was back at painting huge wall installations for his newest collection. The images he sent me were a study in mosaics. He used all manner of textiles, textures, and materials to create his pieces ranging from photographs to rocks to insects.

"Are you ready for your showing next week?" I asked him.

He smiled and my pulse jumped, along with the computer screen. I held my breath, but the screen didn't go out. I let out a sigh. Zane hadn't noticed the technical malfunction. He was too intent on my perfect cheekbones.

"I am," he said. "I arranged … he thought … I wouldn't … showed him."

The screen and sound jumped as he spoke, stuttering along with his answer as I crossed my fingers and toes that the connection didn't break entirely.

The screen froze for more than ten seconds, and my heart plummeted. I closed my eyes. Tears stung the corners, and I let them fall.

"*Nova, êtes-vous là?*"

I opened my eyes at the sound of his voice. "*Oui* —yes. I'm here."

Zane put his pencil down and focused on the screen. He rubbed at the spot where I imagined my tear fell down my cheek, marring its perfection.

The allergy extended to technology as well. Even before satellite communication, when we'd written letters across continents, the letters would get delayed, lost, or damaged when they came into our hands. All signs to remind us that Immortals were not meant to coexist. We ignored them.

"Tell me, *cherie*, what part of history have you saved lately?"

I smiled, swiping the tear from my cheek. "Well, I uncovered a civilization that worshiped monkeys."

"Monkeys? Fascinating."

I laughed. Zane never let me take myself too seriously. He had little interest in history, even where art was concerned. He was much more fascinated with the present moment and finding the beauty within sight. I couldn't blame him. We had lived through terrible times in the past that we'd soon forget. A lot of it, we already *had* forgotten.

It was difficult for humans to carry around a century's worth of their lifespan in their heads. Imagine five hundred years. Over a thousand. More. Immortals were strong, but even our brains couldn't carry that heavy a load. We lost a lot of lifetimes as our brains let go of the past, century by century. The memory loss wasn't chronological. It often had no rhyme or reason.

I remembered watching Rome being built from the period of kings in 600 BCE, but the Renaissance was sketchy to me. I'd spent time in America before Columbus came, but I only knew that because of the records I kept with the Cherokee. Unfortunately, many of the records had been destroyed by pilgrims and conquistadors while I was traveling in India along the Silk Road. I knew I'd been to China, though I had no clear memories of my time there.

No, that wasn't true. I had memories, but they were more like nightmares. It was one of the times I wondered if my brain was protecting me from something I didn't want to remember.

"Someone came to me today with a dragon bone."

"Dragon bone?" Zane rubbed a paint-tipped finger at his square chin. "I thought dinosaurs bored you."

"A dragon bone is an Asian relic. This person, Loren, found it in the Gongyi and needs it deciphered."

Zane let go of his chin and tilted his head to the

side. "You're thinking of going to China? You hate China."

Hate wasn't what I felt when I thought of China. Fear. Shame. Guilt. Those were more fitting emotions.

I always told Zane everything. Everything except why I had an aversion to that particular continent. No one wanted the person they loved to think the worst of them, especially when I wasn't sure what I might have done in the distant past to garner those feelings.

"She thinks there may be a lost civilization," I said.

The corners of his mouth fell. "You will never leave the past buried, will you, my *petite nova*?"

"I would leave it buried if people didn't try to build something new on top of it."

"Ah." He leaned back in his seat. "The plot thickens. Tresor must have building permits on this land."

I felt the hair at the nape of my neck stiffen at the sound of that name. "He's an arrogant asshole with no care for anyone but himself."

Zane shrugged. "I think he sees the world differently than you and me."

I huffed at his charity. "Must you always see the good in people?"

The uptilt to his mouth returned. "I only care about the good in you, *cherie*. The good around you, and the good coming your way."

"You're so good to me," I hedged. "Why don't I come to see you, instead? I'd come to your show. Be a proper girlfriend."

He shook his head as he smiled sadly. "You know what happened the last time. We said we'd wait this time, so we can spend more time together."

Zane and I had spent four months together last year when we met in person. It had put me in the hospital with a case of pneumonia. Once we were separated, I was back on my feet in a few days, but all communication between us was thwarted for weeks. Phones died when we picked them up. Computers short-circuited. Even a mail plane went down. No one was hurt, but all the mail was lost.

"It's just a few more weeks, *nova*," he said. "I'll finish up this showing and then I'm all yours."

I didn't argue because I knew this showing was important to him. I was just being selfish. But I couldn't help it. We were going to live forever, but I got so little of his time in the grand scheme of things.

"Trust me, *mon coeur*, it will be worth the wait."

The tilt at his mouth rose even higher with carnal intent. "You will need all of your strength for what I have planned for you. I'm going to—"

The screen froze. The connection never restored. I stayed on the rooftop staring at his frozen face until the screen and the sky went black.

CHAPTER SIX

The dream began like always. I was dressed in a white gown. It reminded me of a peplos, which were the draped gowns that women in Ancient Greece wore. My feet were bare. I was bound to a stone slab altar. There were men dressed in black, with sashes tied around their waists and hoods covering their faces. They had swords. The moonlight from above caught the glint of their blades. They were everywhere.

I was surrounded. The cold stone permeated the fabric of my gown. My wrists and ankles chafed at the rope abrading my skin. I tugged with all my might, but I couldn't escape.

I was weak. So weak. The worst allergy of my life,

but there were no other Immortals around me. I couldn't understand why my power had failed me.

There was someone holding a jade sword over me. I felt the burning heat of the blade against my skin. The trickle of my blood as it left my wrists.

And then the pain stopped, but the nightmare did not.

More blood splattered, thick droplets suspended in the air. The red liquid caught the moonlight like the steel of the swords. The blood wasn't mine. I saw heads roll, eyes stretched wide, mouths gaped open. Body parts littered the ground—arms, legs, torsos. Not just of the men, but of the women ... and the children.

I opened my mouth to scream, but nothing came out. I bolted up in the bed. My eyes wrenched wide as my hand clenched my throat, raw from my silent screams.

In the hotel room, I poured a glass of water. Then a second. The cold liquid burned my throat. I was fevered, but I was shivering in the cool air.

I looked at the bed like it was an enemy. There was no way I was climbing back under those rumpled sheets. No way I could risk going back to that cold, dark place. I pulled on clothes and slipped outside.

The monuments of the National Mall of the Smithsonian at night were a thing of beauty. The white of the buildings stood out against a cobalt sky. The array of water fountains sprayed a sequence of foaming arcs under yellow lights.

I had been to this land when it was a swamp. Under the cover of night in the face of the history of these multihued, socially diverse, intellectually polarized people, I could admit that progress could be a good thing. But only when it was done right. America had not done everything right, but this culture was a self-reflective one if ever I saw it.

One of Tres Mohandis's signs on a high rise came into view. I cringed. Its steel face went against the white brick motif of the city. It reached up to 130 feet, the max allowed here. The structure looked entirely out of place. The monuments were lovely. But that damn building was an eyesore in the sight line of the museums and monuments, a place I frequented in my line of work. I knew he knew that, and I swore he put it there to antagonize me.

I walked past the Lincoln Memorial to the Reflecting Pool. It was after midnight. D.C. was not New York. This city went to sleep at night. There was hardly a soul on the street. I was alone with only my thoughts to reflect on.

I thought of the bone Loren Van Alst had presented to me today and the story waiting to be revealed. I thought about what Zane had said to me regarding my need to hold on to the past. I wished I could let go of things, but I couldn't. I'd lived a long life, while having to watch so many other lives get snuffed out like candles. I couldn't help but feel it was my duty to record, rescue, and restore as many stories as I could.

Death was easy. It was being erased that scared me.

Wind rustled a ripple in the still waters of the pond. The problem that the breeze presented was the fact that it wasn't a windy night. And so the hairs on the back of my neck prickled. A tickle rose in my throat, but I held on to the cough.

I turned my head to the left. Nothing stirred, not a bird or a beetle. The silence was crushing, like an anchor sinking fast into the depths of the ocean. It wrapped around me and gave a persistent tug downward.

I'd heard drowning was a peaceful way to die, once people stopped struggling. They'd fall into a peaceful sleep as the waters invaded their lungs and shut down their senses, their will, their life.

I inhaled. The cool night air filled my lungs. The

lethargy fled my body, like dirty dishwater swirling down the sink. I was not going anywhere any time soon.

I reached down at my hip for the handle of my sais, only to remember I was in civilization, and it wouldn't do to carry a large blade out in the open. I bent and dug my hands into each of my boots. With the twin daggers in hand, cold steel warmed my palms. I straightened just in time to meet the first attacker.

Only to duck again to miss the sharp edge of a throwing star. The man covered in black had aimed the star true, but I evaded it easily. It had been meant as a momentary distraction while his fists and feet came at me.

I stepped into a reverse lunge, the opposite of what Loren had done at the art gallery. My attacker wasn't an idiot. He was studied in the martial arts.

I continued to step back, step aside, and duck out of his strikes. My evasive maneuvers wouldn't work for long. He landed a kick at my midsection. I grunted.

I wasn't hurt, but the force of his strike knocked some of the wind out of me. He was strong, stronger than most humans. The masked man took a fighting stance. I knew without looking that two other masked men, dressed in black with sashes tied around their waists and hoods covering their faces, had boxed me in on each side.

Had I forgot to mention I was routinely hunted by ninja assassins?

By routinely, I mean they only found me once every decade at best. But they'd been getting better at hunting me. They'd found me more and more frequently during the last hundred years.

Loren had said she'd learned my patterns and it was how she'd found me so easily on the first try. She'd only been following me for a few weeks. These men and their ancestors had been following me for over a thousand years. In the age of technology, they were getting better. Or maybe I was just getting more predictable.

The three ninjas charged, blades gleaming maliciously in the moonlight. It was time to stop playing around. They wouldn't step back, aside, or out of my way. When they struck at me, they were aiming for blood.

About two hundred years ago, they'd overwhelmed me with their sheer force of numbers and bound me. I'd managed to get free of their trap. I might have been outnumbered, but I was still stronger than they were. However, I never wanted to learn where they'd intended to take me. Likely back to that altar in my nightmares.

As three pairs of feet, fists, and blades gunned for me, I dropped down. Once on the ground, I pulled my legs back into my body in a low crouch. I tucked and rolled, striking out my right foot and sweeping the leg of one attacker. Cobra Kai was my spirit guide tonight.

The man tumbled to the ground, still swinging. But I had the advantage of already being low. I jabbed him in the chest with a push kick. The stem of my boot aimed straight for his throat. He staggered backward, bile and blood sputtering out of his mouth. He fell to his knees, then keeled over.

I didn't have time to take pride in my precise blow. The other two ninjas loomed over me, blades at the ready. I sent a dagger toward the heart of one. He turned, and it caught his shoulder. Not a second later, I sent the other blade to follow it. This one landed in his ear. The man blinked in surprise and fell to the ground.

By then, I was on my feet. I met the strikes and kicks of the third man blow for blow. He caught a lucky shot in my rib with his booted instep. The blow rattled me. He was strong, superhumanly so. But I was stronger.

I took a flying leap that landed me on the other side of the Reflecting Pool. The third man took the same gravity-defying, fifty-meter leap across the waters. But he was wounded, so he fell short and landed in the water.

I paused for a second. Waiting to see if, like in the high-wire martial arts films, he could run across the water. The water was less than two feet deep. The calves of his pants were soaked through as he charged toward me.

I had the time to flee, but I didn't run. I couldn't. They would only come after me again. And then again.

The last ninja standing came at me, thrusting his dagger at my torso. The blade sliced through the air, narrowly missing my neck. I turned with his motion and then delivered a roundhouse kick that connected under his raised arm. A second, lower kick shattered his kneecap. Finally, a punch to the jaw sent him off balance.

I reached for the dagger, pinning his shoulders to the ground with my knees. Holding the weapon at his heart with one hand, I unmasked him with the other.

That was a mistake. In the movies, no one mourned the faceless ninja horde that fell like flies under the hero's hand. When their masks are removed, people are reminded of their humanity. This man looked to be in his early thirties, Asian, with dark eyes.

"Why are you here?" I asked him.

He glared at me, but he didn't answer. They never answered. Each one took whatever he knew about me and my past to the death. These were the men of my nightmares. I had hoped for centuries that their attacks were what my nightmares were made from, and not that I had birthed the nightmare born of actions I couldn't remember.

I took a deep breath and voiced part of what I'd learned from Loren's dragon bone. It was a phrase I had no knowledge of. But just because I didn't know it didn't mean I hadn't lived it before.

"Is it the Lin Kuie?"

The ninja's eyes sparked at the words I'd translated from the dragon bone. The English translation was akin to *forest ghost*. Something whispered in my mind, but I couldn't grab hold of the memory.

"Do you know what that means?" I asked.

He only glared. I readied the blade, not expecting him to speak, so my grip loosened when he did.

"The blood of my ancestors is on your hands," he said. "We will not stop until we trade your bones for our blood."

He swiped the blade out of my hand and reversed our position, slashing the business side of the blade across my shirt. A gaping wound spread across the cotton, exposing my lace bra.

The man froze as he looked down at my skin, copping a look at my girls. I elbowed him in the face for the destruction of my shirt and the sneak peek. The dagger fell out of his hand. When my fist came back, I felt the tug of broken skin.

I looked down at the growing trail of red that wept from my chest and realized it was my blood that had transfixed him. He reached again for the weapon, but I beat him to it. With one slash, I gutted him like he'd done to my shirt. Then I let the blade fall out of my hands and rolled onto my back.

Dammit. It looked like I'd be making a trip to China after all.

CHAPTER SEVEN

The wound on my chest smarted as I reached for the controls. A human would've needed stitches for such a deep gash, but my skin had already begun knitting itself back together overnight. In the noonday sun, it looked like a week's worth of healing had happened in only twelve hours. I disengaged the autopilot and began my approach. The safety harness gave no purchase and restrained my chest, causing the abraded skin to protest.

I wasn't used to pain. It was such an infrequent experience in my long life. I'd heard women talk about how men could never handle childbirth or menstrual cramps. I didn't have a menstrual cycle, which meant I would never have children, but also that I'd never experience either a cramp or a contraction. Hell, I'd rarely experienced a paper cut. So a wound along my torso, albeit a rapidly healing one, was a lot to manage along with flying a seaplane.

I loved flying. Loved flying more than driving. But I loved driving more than sailing. It was all about the speed for me. Planes could reach speeds that would leave cars in the dust and boats in the wake.

I would never be able to count the days of my life, but I did enjoy watching the tick of a speedometer. I loved the wind in my hair. I craved wide-open spaces where I could run, fly, sail, and whizz past life in the blink of an eye.

Pulling back the throttle, I heard and felt the sound of the engines give over power. I pulled the yoke and leveled the aircraft to the horizon. The plane made a smooth descent toward the crystal-blue waters of the Caribbean Sea.

Up ahead, I saw my home, my island. It was shaped like my name, my real name. A sandy beach jutted out on three sides, forming the bottom half of a box with an open top. In the center was a dense forest of green-topped trees. At the top of the island was a small mountain. The mountain range extended from the tip of the sandy beach and then sliced diagonally into the forest, cutting through some of the trees.

From above, the island looked like the letter U with a divot curling inward at the top right corner. Or, more aptly, like the number nine in Hebrew and Aramaic. That was me. And this was my island.

I called the island Noohra. The word was an ancient Galilean form of the word "light." A young philosopher I'd befriended nearly two thousand years ago had called knowledge "the light." He'd postulated that if humans were the repositories of knowledge, then we were the light of the world. He'd gone out to spread that gospel and was crucified for his preachings.

The small seaplane came in for a landing in the water. My tiny island of light was out in the middle of nowhere where no one would find it. Humans would nail me to a cross for the knowledge this place contained. I'd found the island when I'd been on a pirate ship in the early 1500s.

I'd been sailing back from the New World, as the British liked to call it in those times. I'd been in what would later be called the state of Florida. My skin coloring was decidedly darker than a European woman's, but the slave trade hadn't begun at that point. Still, travel wasn't exactly safe for me. But I was stronger than any man I met, and they soon learned to keep a respectable distance or they permanently lost the use of their family jewels.

On a journey back to Spain, the ship was commandeered by pirates. Unfortunately for the pirates, I was aboard the ship. I singlehandedly dispensed the pirates of their captain, first mate, and half the crew. For my troubles, my shipmates labeled me a witch.

The mob was able to shove me off the ship into the shark-infested waters. I made it aboard the pirate ship. The frightened crew decided to take their chances with the sharks instead of a witch. I sailed a few days, coming close to what felt like death before I found my island. It came at me out of the horizon like a city of light.

There were no locals who could happen upon the island without a motorized boat or a seaplane. If they did come upon it by chance, then they would have to walk through a mile of deep forest, and then another of swamp, in order to reach any of the treasures hidden within.

I made my way inland, walking slower than I normally would as every step tugged at the torn skin on my chest.

This was my fortress of solitude. It was where I came to rejuvenate. The place that refueled me. The one spot in the world where I left my blades at the door.

I reached the structure hidden at the base of the mountain. It was there that I'd built a cabin. I pulled the strap over my shoulder that held my bush sword. It was the same case from Honduras. I'd had the strap repaired while in D.C. I bent over, sliding my hands in my boots to extract the twin daggers I'd used last night in my battle with the ninjas. I'd cleaned the blades of blood after I deposited the three bodies where they might never be found in the polluted waters of the Anacostia River. Next, I released the sais that swung in a holster on my hip.

The beauty of piloting my own plane was that I didn't have to argue with TSA about my weapons. No, I wasn't expecting an air battle. Nor was I expecting to meet anyone on the grounds of my secret hiding space. But I had needed the comfort of the steel after the ordeal from last night.

I entered my sanctuary with empty hands, bare feet, and a weary spirit. Once I activated the solar-powered generator, my inner sanctum illuminated. Instantly, I felt lighter.

It had taken me nearly two hundred years to

build the compound and move my trove here. I often came here after spending time with Zane. Partly because I was physically weak, but mostly because I was emotionally vulnerable. Leaving Zane was always as hard on my spirit as it was on my body. In those times, I liked to surround myself with my treasures.

I went deeper into the cabin. There were only two rooms. A space with a desk for me to write and work, and a smaller room with a large four-poster bed made from the tree trunks of the island's interior.

On the desk was the last artifact I was working on. There were three scrolls encased in protective glass sitting out in the open on the table. The scrolls had been found in the Qumran Caves near the Dead Sea in the West Bank of the Jordan River. There had been hundreds of such scrolls found at the site in the middle of the last century. Most were now on display in museums. But these three spoke of twelve beings, men and women of great power, who never aged and never died.

I'd taken the scrolls from the site and disappeared into the night before anyone could question me. And no, that wasn't tomb raiding. First off, the scrolls were in a cave. Secondly, I didn't sell the knowledge off to the highest bidder. Because, thirdly and most importantly, this was knowledge that would be dangerous if it were shared with the world.

The scrolls had a good bit of detail on each of the twelve Immortals. I was trying to figure out who wrote the scrolls. It hadn't been me. The current theory about the Qumran scrolls, or, as they were more commonly known, the Dead Sea Scrolls, was that they were written by the Essenes, which was a Jewish sect that had lived around Qumran centuries ago.

I had my doubts. In any case, I couldn't focus on that mystery now. I had another to solve.

I walked through the work area and past the bedroom until I came to the door of my vault. Releasing the latch, I opened the door and began the descent into the interior of the mountain.

There was a reason why wine was kept inside underground caves, why many artifacts were found in pristine condition inside mountain caves. Caves were air-tight, conserved energy, and held cool temperatures.

I'd built shelves and units in my cave of knowledge. Like in a library, I'd organized things according to subject, culture, and era. I'd been using the system before Melvil Dewey ever learned his ABCs.

There was a host of texts from the decimated tomes of the Library of Alexandria. I hadn't been able to save everything from the destruction, but I had gotten out the original canon of the Bible and the schematics of the Great Pyramid. The walls of my caves were lined with scrolls and tomes from further back than my mind could remember.

I admit, I might be a bit of a hoarder. But there was not one single thing in this cave that could be thrown away. These were also the treasures I thought better than to share with the rest of the world. There was some knowledge that was dangerous to mankind. My friend Yeshua had found that out when he tried to share the light of his knowledge. He was betrayed by his friends and his hands were nailed to a cross.

I'd dedicated my life to the preservation of history, cultures, and people. I didn't fear death. How could I as a person who rarely felt pain or weakness?

Death was a loose concept to me. Nothing ever truly died. The dirt rebirthed and recycled everything and everyone. Yeshua had been reborn a prophet, and his knowledge was still spread across the world today.

But I'd also watched cultures be erased. Seen knowledge razed to the ground. I'd witnessed people be whited out. I'd observed history be rewritten. Being erased was the worst thing I could imagine.

After I sat down inside my cave, I pored through my personal diaries of world history, starting with the volumes I had on Asia. I had written about the Shang Dynasty and my time in what would become Mongolia. The Shang Dynasty lasted from 1600 to 1046 BCE. My written accounts of the Zhou Dynasty, who'd come after the Shang, and their medical progress were there. But there was nothing about the Xia tribe who had purportedly come before these two great cultures. Not a single word or reference. Just a gaping void in the historical timeline.

I closed the volumes and tried to open my mind. Shutting my eyes, I pulled darkness around me to focus. Had I ripped out those pages of history? But I would never do that. No matter how ugly a history, no matter how vile a truth, I always told the stories. Without fail, I kept the records no one wanted unearthed. Unfailingly, I got my fingers dirty in the mire of the past.

I let go of the blackness and opened my eyes to

the dim light of the cave. There was nothing in my mind or on the page.

I hadn't written down a single account of the ninja attacks over the centuries. Even now, my hand shook as I recalled the details of the one last night. I could write in every language known to mankind; I could read them all too. But I couldn't form a single character about any of these attacks. Nor did I have a single account of the Xia.

There had to be something more going on. Realizing I couldn't handle this on my own anymore, I decided to go to the one person who I thought might have some answers.

CHAPTER EIGHT

"Sister Una is in the gardens," the young nun said to me in a voice that was barely above a whisper. She wore a coif that reminded me of an origami bird. The hat folded into a triangle over her forehead and the tips stuck out at the side like wings. Her Spanish cant told me she was from poverty.

In the early days of convents, the Church only accepted girls from wealthy families. These girls came with dowries that would be passed on to the Church. Sometimes the girls who came were young women with babes in arms. Other times, they were widows who chose to live a quiet life of service after the deaths of their husbands. In the old times, a convent was rarely a woman's first choice.

This morning, there had been only a few sisters about the halls in the worn-down building. Descending the cracked stone steps into a barren garden, I saw Sister Una, as she was calling herself these days, in the distance. She'd removed her habit, exposing her bare neck and shoulders to the warm Catalina sunshine. Sister Una was not poor, a widow, or young. And she'd had many options to live in other places, do other things, and be someone different. But being here was her choice.

A tickle struck the back of my throat as I walked through the blooms closer to the woman. On her back was a marking that looked like a cursive number four. In the ancient lettering, it was the first mark—aleph. I rolled my shoulder, feeling the phantom of a similar mark on my shoulder blade.

With a spade in her hand, the nun dug up a vegetable. A mole as large as her hand came along with it. The creature tried to squirm away, but the nun caught it and held it tight within her deceptively delicate-looking hands. The mole bit its sharp teeth into the spot between her thumb and forefinger, barely breaching the rough skin of the webbing between her fingers.

As I came a few steps closer, I felt the healed skin at my chest tingle at the proximity to another of my kind. The mole struck again. This time, there was a tear in that patch of skin. The nun winced, but it wasn't from pain. It was curiosity.

"Why are you disturbing my peace, Tisa?"

"It's good to see you too, Aleph."

With her free hand, Aleph reached out for a ball of twine, then tethered the screeching, struggling mole until it was immobile. After that, she took a moment to examine her hand. It was only the tiniest of pinpricks now, but she stared at it as though it were something big and important.

"If you believe the stories, we were born in a garden," she said, motioning around the barren garden with her uninjured hand.

Aleph believed that Immortals were the children of angels. She was waiting for our forefathers to return and collect us. Aleph figured since they'd marked us with numbers, they'd return for us. It was why she was in a convent. Though nuns were said to marry God, she was waiting for a ride home to wherever she thought that might be. I no longer believed in Heaven, Hell, or gods.

"In the original canonical works of the Bible," Aleph said, her voice quiet, "it says the Nephilim were on the earth in those days—and afterward— when the sons of God went to the daughters of men and had children by them. They were the heroes of old, men of renown, Genesis 6:4."

Aleph was the oldest of us. But her angelic round face and thin body made her look like she'd just graduated high school. She turned to me, her movements slow and languid. Her eyes were the color of the sky after a storm, an eerie peace over a wasteland of destruction. I didn't like having her attention on me, but I needed answers, so I held still and returned her gaze.

"That last line, I think it was mistranslated," Aleph said. "Because I was born first and not a man. You wouldn't happen to know where I could find an original copy of the Bible? Would you, Tisa?"

"They were destroyed in the Library of Alexandria. You remember that, Aleph."

"Hmm," she said, turning her attention back to the mole.

Immortals kept secrets, and we lied. It was for self-preservation when we did it to one another. It was for the survival of us all when we did it to humans. In the past, when humans knew about us, they'd hunted us down and either worshiped, tried to kill, or experimented on us. Sometimes all three.

We'd been worshiped as gods. Egyptian gods—us. Greek gods—yup. Some of us liked to play at monarch, but because we didn't age, it made humans suspicious. So instead of taking the crown and scepter in hand, the power-hungry among us became advisors, whispering in the ears of queens, dictators, prime ministers, and presidents.

"Do you like it here, Aleph?"

"It's the same as every convent."

"You moved not too long ago," I said.

Aleph moved convents every twenty years or so when the other sisters and monks saw that her baby face didn't age. Though she was the oldest of us, she appeared younger than we did. And somehow, she held on to many of her early memories. Maybe that was what made her a touch crazy.

"Were you not safe in the last place?"

"Why do you ask, child?" Aleph wrinkled her brow as the still waters pooled in her dilated pupils. "Do you need safe haven?"

Most Immortals were well-practiced in the art of the redirect. Aleph was the master. She had patience and cunning. I had some of that, too, when it came to a treasure buried in the dirt. But when it came to people, I was usually a quick-triggered bulldozer.

"Have you heard any of the legends of the Lin Kuie?"

Aleph frowned. "I don't know that word. Is it some new slang the youth are slinging?"

"It means forest ghost. Some believe they were the original ninjas." I'd done a little reading on the commercial plane ride over from the Caribbean to Europe. There wasn't much on the actual Lin Kuie in the recorded human history either. It seemed that modern-day gamers had appropriated the term for characters in their video games.

"Ninjas? You mean the Orientals who leap about in their pajamas?" Aleph chuckled like an eighty-year-old woman. It looked sinister on the face of a girl who appeared eighteen. "Are you hunting flying men who dance in the dark? You need only go to the picture shows."

Aleph turned away from me. Without preamble, she took her garden shears and sliced the mole from navel to nose. The creature let out a toe-curling scream. I looked away, my eyes burning. My stomach roiled.

Death, I could handle. Needless suffering, I couldn't abide.

"I've lived every experience in this world, except this one," Aleph said as the mole ceased its screeching and its body went still. Its eyes turned glassy and lifeless, just like hers.

There was a moment of silence. But it was only my silence that was out of respect. The silence ended with the thunk of the mole's body being returned unceremoniously to the dirt. I looked off into the patch where its body had landed, forever silenced. No one would tell its story.

"There's something after me," I said. "Some people. At least, I think they're part human. I feel weakened when they're near, like it's one of us." I opened my shirt. The wound had healed. The deep gash that had sliced my chest was now only a faint scar. "One of them did this."

Aleph came up and put her cold hands on my shoulders. I tried to hold still, but I shuddered. I had seen many inexplicable things in my times. There were other kinds of magic in this world besides us.

As far as I knew, there were twelve Immortals who walked the earth. We found evidence of ourselves throughout recorded history and references to our likenesses in stories told about the times before. But we weren't the only supernatural beings who walked this planet.

Somehow, these ninjas knew about me. It could've come from my own mouth or from someone else's. Zane had never mentioned being attacked by ninjas, but then again, neither had I.

It could be another Immortal. Not all of them liked me. Namely, Tres. But I'd interfered in other Immortals' business as well. Immortals had gone to war with one another, but it rarely came to physical assaults. Only we could do true harm to one another. If we happened to kill one of our kind, well, then, that was it. No one wanted a murder like that hanging over their head, because the next Immortal could do it to them.

"They're strong, all Asian males," I said. "They remain in human form, so not shifters. Could they be demons?"

"Demons have no interest in us. They want souls."

Aleph didn't believe we had souls. She believed that was why we didn't die.

I pulled the dagger from my bag. Her eyebrows rose with interest. I wasn't sure if the interest was in the blade or what the blade could offer her. The blade should not have torn my skin. At least not without another Immortal present. Being impervious to harm was a perk of living forever.

I knew the ninjas attacking me weren't immortal because I'd killed them, many of them. But they were strong, they made me feel weak, and they could wound me. And they kept coming, generation after generation, which meant they were being born and taught.

"I was alone—no other Immortals were present. I was struck with this and bled." I handed her the blade.

When her eyes lit up, I wondered if I had made a mistake. My flesh was vulnerable in her presence. I didn't think Aleph would kill me. She was more interested in her own death. Plus, I wouldn't hold still like the mole.

"Aleph, is there a substance that could kill us? Or a special metal? This blade breached my skin."

She sniffed the blade. Then she stuck out her tongue and tasted the metal.

"Maybe a witch's magic?" I suggested.

There were objects in this world that held power. Witches were those who could sense and wield that power.

"There is no magic, only blood." Aleph rolled her tongue around the roof of her mouth and closed her eyes. "No, not blood. Bone."

That made even less sense. I tried to smooth my face from the grossness of her action by the time she opened her eyes and refocused on me. "Have you heard anything similar from any of the other twelve?"

"You mean ten."

Had she forgotten some of us? There were twelve Immortals. We didn't have much occasion to meet, especially with the allergy. I didn't keep tabs on everyone. The only Immortals I saw regularly were Zane, every few months; Aleph, every decade or so; and Delta a few times a century. We weren't exactly a family.

"Didn't you know? Epsilon and Vau fancied themselves in love. They paired up and went off to live ever after, happily I suppose. But I haven't seen them in over two thousand years."

Vague images of the two came to mind. I couldn't remember the last time I'd seen them. "You think they're ... dead?" The word sounded foreign on my tongue, which was familiar with nearly every word known. But referring to death and an Immortal was an unfamiliar concept.

"They probably grew weak and died of old age." Aleph said it in a dreamy voice. "How is Zayin, by the way?"

She ran the blade over her finger, watching the blood leak out of her skin with fascination.

"Aleph, have I ever told you anything I've done that was ... bad?"

Asking an Immortal about their memories was

like asking a potential partner about their sexual history on the first date. You weren't sure if what they told you was the truth, and they likely underestimated their experience to make themselves look good.

"Good and bad are such human notions. What was bad one century is good in another. I've spent so much time making amends for the terrible things I've done in the past, only to wake up a thousand years later and no one even remembers, including me. I don't concern myself with such human trifles anymore."

She tucked the blade in the folds of her tunic and smiled up at me. I knew I wouldn't get it back. I wondered if I should worry about what she might do with it.

"Forgive yourself, Tisa. You are the only one to lay the blame."

No, she was wrong. It was a few hundred ninjas and me.

I knew I wasn't going to get anything useful from her, so I made to leave.

"Off to see your lover?" Aleph said. "If you see Epsilon and Vau, pray give them my regards."

CHAPTER NINE

The woman pulled out a thin blade and reached for my hand. I took a deep breath and uncrossed my arms. With another breath, I wrung out my hands, shaking my fingers loose from the clench they held. Finally, I gave the woman my right hand.

"Square or rounded?" she asked, readying the nail file for work.

"Rounded squares," I answered, resting my left hand on the armrest of the salon chair.

The nail technician began to work on my pinkie finger, and I relaxed into the rolling pins and vibrations of the massage chair. The visit with Aleph the other day had left me tense and out of sorts. She always left me feeling exposed. Aleph looked at me as though she knew more than she let on, and she liked to talk in riddles.

Despite the way I made my living, searching for the lands of the lost and deciphering old scrolls, I hated riddles. In my everyday life, I preferred things to be simple and straightforward. Like the controls of a cockpit.

I'd chartered a plane in Spain— an SJ30 SyberJet —and flew it solo to China. The cost of the aircraft wasn't an issue. I had thousands of years of gems, coins, cash, and credit at my disposal. What was priceless were the demands on my mind and body courtesy of a solo flight across continents.

The journey had taken half the day. I was mentally and physically exhausted by the end of it, which had been the point. The flight had taken my mind off my plight.

I was looking forward to lugging myself to my hotel room and crawling under the covers for a full day before figuring out my next move. But first, I had to do something about my cuticles and chipped nail polish. A girl had to have her priorities in order, after all.

"I thought I'd find you here."

I turned my head to see Loren Van Alst slide into the cushioned salon chair next to me. A petite Asian woman scooted up on a rolling chair with a tray of nail polishes. Loren selected a coral color, discarded her heels, and dipped a toe in the sudsy water.

The Beijing airport salon was not what Loren had led me to believe. It was a couple of massage chairs with foot baths. Pretty much a standard neighborhood nail salon. But I wasn't complaining. The water on my feet had been welcome. And now the polish on my fingernails was presentable despite my chewing at them from stress over the past couple of days.

"How did you know I was coming today?" I asked Loren.

"I'd been looking to see if you used the ticket I reserved for you." Loren gave the nail tech her left foot. "When you didn't, I thought you might be flying coach." She shuddered, shimmying her chest and wiggling her hips at the mention of the back of a plane.

"I said I wasn't coming at all."

Loren snorted. "I saw your eyes when you saw my photograph. You're an artifact junkie. You weren't going to pass up the chance to get your hands on that bone."

She flounced back in her seat and moaned with delight as the nail tech scrubbed at her heels.

"And then this morning," Loren continued, "I saw there was a private plane coming in piloted by someone called Nova Flueve. What's the translation, again? New River? Nine River?"

Loren turned to me. I avoided her gaze. She'd figured out the key to my aliases. Either she was as good as she claimed with patterns, or I really was getting predictable in my old age. I wasn't usually this paranoid, but I was walking into the lion's den. The men who attacked me were likely born and bred on this continent. They wouldn't have to travel far to throw a dagger or aim a kick at me.

"Anyway, you're here now," Loren said. "And you're just in time. I've arranged a meeting with the antiquities expert tonight."

I tilted my head as I regarded her. "Those meetings aren't easy to get. How'd you manage that?"

Loren arched her back. "I have a lot of assets." She gave her bra straps a tug and then let go. They snapped back with an indecent crack against her chest.

I tapped my freshly painted toes on the top of the basin. "Loren, we're scientists. Our greatest weapon is our mind, not our breasts."

"Not when the problem before us is a man." She

shrugged. "And an old lover. But we broke it off on good terms. I told him I needed a favor."

"And he told you to come by for a meeting?"

She cocked her head to the side. "I'm not sure. We got disconnected."

The chime of a phone interrupted my comeback. I looked down and was shocked to see Zane's number. His unscheduled calls rarely came through.

"Problem?" Loren asked.

"Boyfriend."

"Oh." Loren wrinkled her nose. She frowned, twisting her lip in disappointment.

"What?" I demanded, my hackles going up.

"I didn't take you for a monogamist."

I adjusted my pants and stood, moving over to the drying section since I was done. Answering my phone, I said, "Zane?"

Part of me didn't expect to hear him, but his voice came through crystal clear, like he was standing right next to me. "I didn't expect to catch you, *mon coeur*. I thought you would be immersed in the muds of a spa in Catalina."

I'd texted Zane that I was going to Catalina. The region happened to have excellent spas. Technically, I had been in the mud when I walked through the convent gardens. But I hadn't had any beauty treatments. All in all, it wasn't *exactly* a lie.

And I was in a spa now. "I just got my nails done." I looked around the airport salon in the heart of Beijing.

"What color?" His voice hit a low register, like it would if he'd asked what I was wearing.

"You're a pervert." I giggled. "Why can I hear you so well?"

"Delta stopped by."

"Oy, Nia," came a smoke-filled voice in the distance.

"Heyyy, Delta." I dragged out the syllables of my salutation.

"The transmission is crazy clear, isn't it?" Delta shouted in the background.

"She's created some kind of gadget that's given me a signal boost," Zane said, coming back on the line.

"She gave you a boost, did she?" I tapped my painted nail on the back of the phone case. "Wasn't that nice of her…"

I really had no reason to be irritated. Delta was a tech geek and one of the few Immortals I would call a friend. She'd also lost any interest in males a millennium or so ago. My jealousy stemmed from any Immortal who spent time with Zane. If they were around him zapping his energy, that meant less time for me when I finally got to see him.

Zane chuckled instead of addressing my snark. "I asked Delta for the use of her wares…"

He chuckled again at my audible exhale of annoyance.

"…because I have some good news. They restored the cottage."

"Wait? Do you mean *the* cottage?"

"Yes, the cottage in Nice where we spent our first month together."

Zane had pursued me for decades. During that time, he never pushed or imposed himself upon me. He'd always approached me with that same confident swagger. When I rejected him time and time again, he'd offer a patient smile with a glint in his eyes that promised me a next time.

We ran into each other repeatedly during the Protestant Reformation. I was sequestering away artwork deemed immoral by the church. He was painting and sculpting more of it to put on display in defiance. At the time, I refused to admit I admired him for it. It was during my stay in Versailles, under the reign of Louis XIV, who commissioned hundreds of pieces of artwork, music, and literature, that I finally gave Zane any attention.

In the spring, I sat still for him in the Palace of Versailles while he painted my portrait. In the winter, I saw him again in Paris and stood in the snow while he kissed me first on one cheek, then another, and then on my lips. In the summer in a cottage in Nice, I'd given him my body. By the fall, he had my heart.

"It'll be open in two weeks, and I got us the first booking," he was saying. "Right after my showing. This means we'll see each other sooner, as you wished. And we can stay for a whole month."

"Oh..." I sighed.

"Oh?" he parroted.

"I might not be able to make it in two weeks."

"Spain isn't that far from France, the last time I checked a map."

I picked at the peeling Formica on the drying station's counter. "I'm actually in China."

The phone heated in my hand. I heard something that sounded like a light bulb splinter on his end. There was silence on the line. I worried we'd lost the connection. But then I heard him inhale and sigh.

"You're going on the excavation with the Van Alst woman?"

I nodded, then realized he couldn't see me. "At least to stop Tres from building on the site before it can be excavated."

There was more silence on the line.

"What about our time together?" he asked.

"It doesn't have to be in the cottage," I said. "We could meet in a grungy motel, and I'd be happy. I just need to see this through first."

"Tell me why, Nova. Why is this artifact so important?"

His voice was so soft. It urged the truth from me.

I was so close to telling him. I wondered if I would have in that moment if we were alone and I didn't have a nosy Dutch woman behind me, most certainly eavesdropping. "I just need to know how this story ended. Can you understand that?"

"No." He sighed, but there was no bite to his denial. "I'm a selfish man. I only care about our story. But I care more for your happiness, you know that."

"You make me happy." I cradled the phone in my hand, pressing the receiver closer to my mouth as though I could kiss him.

This world we lived in was filled with ugly, dark things. I spent my life digging up the evidence of that fact. And every time I found something disheartening, Zane would pull out his colors and paint me a dream world—a beautiful fantasy. I didn't think I could go on every day without the beauty he showed me. I couldn't remember how I did before I met him.

"I know I make you happy," he said. "I am an old, dusty thing with lost stories to uncover."

I giggled again. And then, "Zane? Do you remember Epsilon and Vau?"

The line crackled. We were obviously testing the boundaries of Delta's signal boost.

"What made you think of them?" he asked.

"I saw Aleph."

"I didn't know you still visited her."

"I check on her every couple of decades. She's so preoccupied with death. I guess I just want to make sure she's still with us. She's living in a convent in Catalina now."

"That woman is a menace, if to no one other than herself. I don't like you being near her."

I jerked away from the phone, my spine going rigid. "Are you telling me to stay away from her?"

Zane chuckled. "I'm a wise old man. I would never presume to tell Dr. Nia Rivers what to do. But I do hope you take my counsel, *mon coeur*. I have respect for my elders, but Aleph is on the edge of crazy. She likes to play games like Bet and Yod."

"I think she remembers more than she lets on."

"I'm certain she does. Why do you mention Epsilon and Vau?"

"Just something she said."

"I remember them," Zane said. "They were very much in love."

"You speak of them in the past."

"I haven't seen or heard from them in a long time."

"Do you think they're dead?"

He didn't answer.

"Do you think that could happen to us if we stay together too long? That we'd weaken and die?"

"No," he said before I finished speaking. "We're careful. We have a system. I'm going to love you until the end of time, Nova."

My heart warmed at the declaration. And suddenly, I couldn't remember why I'd flown to the opposite side of the world rather than landing in France to be in this man's arms.

"And, Nova..."

But the phone crackled. The connection fizzled. The line snapped. And the phone died.

CHAPTER TEN

I stepped out of the hotel later that evening. Unlike in D.C., the Beijing skyline was completely obstructed by the hand of human progress. Steel buildings scraped the sky. Most of nature was covered in concrete. The evening looked like a cloudy day with smog visible in the pale moonlight. Not a single star was visible under the array of neon light that shone across the horizon.

There were Starbucks and McDonald's amid the pagodas. Construction sites mixed in with rundown temples and steel high rises. A wrecking ball hung in front of a temple. On the beam of the ball, written in bold block letters, was the name Mohandis Enterprises. The man was literally bulldozing his way through this culture.

Out on the streets, people were dressed in modern garb, more futuristic than anything with glossy fabrics. No one was in black with covered faces. But I was still unsettled walking down the streets of Beijing.

"Hey." A hand reached out and grabbed at my elbow.

In two seconds, with two flicks of my wrist, my blade landed against Loren's neck.

A half second later, the tip of her cane dug into my rib cage. We were in a tight clench. No one could see the weapons unless they peered between us. Her eyebrows were raised, not in fear but in a question.

We stared each other down, neither of us saying a word. Neither of us backing off.

"I don't like being snuck up on," I offered instead of an apology.

She nodded slowly while pursing her lips. "So, no surprise birthday parties for you, then."

I lowered the blade. She retracted the cane.

Wiping at the tiny nick at her neck, I said, "I have some concealer in my purse."

I took out my makeup kit and applied a dusting on the damage I'd caused to her skin. She held still, eyeing me curiously, but she didn't ask why I wore a blade beneath my skirt. Probably for the same reason I didn't ask why she carried a cane in her purse.

"Cute dress," Loren said after I put my makeup case away.

Most of the wardrobe in my luggage consisted of all-weather cargo pants, moisture-wicking shirts, and worn hiking boots. But I always made room for a little black dress.

"Thanks," I said. "Yours too."

My dress was simple, damn near plain compared to Loren's. It hugged my bust and flared over my hips to allow my legs freedom of movement, if I needed it. Loren's dress looked like it was held up by a wing and a prayer. Each time she inhaled, the spindly straps stretched as though they would snap at any moment to release what she claimed were her best assets. She grinned at me like she knew it.

"I still don't understand why we're wearing cocktail dresses to a business meeting," I said.

Loren waggled her head and pursed her lips again. "It's not exactly a business meeting, more of a party."

We fell into step as we headed down the crowded street. My eyes darted right and left, taking in the sights and sounds. It was sensory overload after being out in the middle of a jungle with silent soldiers and focused scientists, and then in a convent of praying nuns.

"Party?" I asked.

This time, Loren lifted one shoulder before she answered. "More of a festival."

"Festival?" I put my hand on her forearm to stop her forward motion. People bumped into us as they tried to reroute their steps on the crowded sidewalk. "Loren, do we actually have a meeting with an official from SACH?"

SACH stood for State Administration of Cultural Heritage. They were responsible for conserving and protecting China's historical locations.

"It's not a scheduled sit-down," Loren said slowly, as though explaining complex math to a grade-schooler. "But my contact will be there, and we can meet with him."

"Contact? You mean your ex-boyfriend?"

"Ew." She shuddered. "I don't do boyfriends. He's a former lover. And I told you, we left it on good terms."

I sighed, wondering what I was walking into. I could just ditch Loren and head down to the Gongyi on my own. But then I'd spend who knew how long just trying to find the site. I decided I could stick it out for the night. Besides, I needed a party to help loosen the last dregs of stress from my bones.

"It'll be fun," Loren said. "It's a dynastic festival with performances from the Shang and Zhou Dynasties. They even have a performance from the Xia."

"I thought the Xia still weren't a recognized dynasty?"

"That's what we're here to change. That's what you do, right? Save lost cultures. You're the Wonder Woman of history."

I snorted, but I let her lead me across the street. She ushered me through the gates of a park. There were white tents set up around smaller pavilions outlined with red and gold flags. Men and women milled around with glasses of wine in their hands, their evening finery cloaked in an air of privilege.

"*Ni hao*, Li," Loren said.

A tall, waifish man in a tailored suit turned around. His eyes met with Loren's bust, and his nostrils flared. Then his gaze tilted up to her face, and he cringed.

"The answer is no, Ms. Van Alst." Li gave a

definitive shake of his head and sliced the air with his hand.

"Since when did I become *Ms.* Van Alst?"

"Since you nearly caused an international incident the last time you went onto the Mohandis construction site in Gongyi. Without permission, I might add."

"I had permission … your permission." Loren breathed in, her chest swelling. "Which I need again."

Li's eyes dipped down to the straps of Loren's dress. One of the spaghetti straps quivered. The edge of his eye twitched along with it. He shut his eyes. "No."

Loren frowned. Her chin hit her chest. She eyed her boobs as though something was wrong. I covered my mouth to hide my snort.

"You're just using me," Li was saying. "I nearly lost my job because of you when we were dating."

Loren scratched at her temple and screwed up her eyes in confusion. "Dating?"

"I still haven't forgotten about the Daqian painting that was in SACH's possession last year when we were together. It had been authenticated when it came into our possession, but when it was sold, it was determined to be a fake."

"An awful fake at that. A child could've painted a better copy." Loren's lip curled up. She caught my eye, averted her gaze, and turned back to Li. "Besides, it's a bone, not a painting this time. This is Dr. Nia Rivers, world-renowned artifact authenticator. She says the bone is authentic."

Li turned to me. "You've seen this dragon bone she's going on about?"

"Well…" I began and stopped.

"She's seen the picture," Loren said. "And from that, she believes its authenticity. Now, if we can just get clearance to get down onto the land with a few of your people on our team—"

Li shook his head again, definitively this time. "I can't trust your word. Your father was a good forger, and you have his talents. I can't take that risk, no matter the reward."

Loren's grip tightened on her bag. I put my hand on her forearm. I was stronger than her, but I felt the strength of anger coursing through her. Luckily, Li wound himself back into the crowd before she could produce her cane.

"Blind asshole," Loren spat. "He has the find of a lifetime in his grasp, and he won't trouble himself to do the work to get his hands dirty."

"Is that what you call leaving a relationship on good terms?" I asked.

Loren scratched at her cheek and screwed up her eyes in confusion. "Relationship?"

I chuckled despite myself, but then I sobered. "Loren, did you forge a Daqian landscape painting?"

Zhang Daqian was a renowned painter of splashed landscapes and lotus drawings. Many in the world might not know his name, but they could see his paintings in Chinese restaurants and copies on everything from calendars to wallpaper.

"No," she said. She scratched at her nose, reminding me of the story of Pinocchio. Huffing, she turned to me with her hands on her hips. "Do you really care about a couple of watercolor paintings? Or do you want to get your hands on that dragon bone?"

My forehead wrinkled as I squinted at this woman before me. She was a definite tomb raider, an alleged art forger, and a likely liar. But she was also my only lead to finding out more about the Lin Kuie and what I'd been doing in China nearly two thousand years ago.

"So what's the plan now?" I asked. "Do you have another way in?"

Loren's eyes lit with mischief. But before she

could hatch whatever new harebrained scheme that had come into her head, someone called out to her.

"Ms. Van Alst, is that you?"

We turned to see a slight man. There was a hunch to his back. His white hair was in wisps. But his smile, which wobbled as it spread, was wide and infectious.

"Dr. Nia Rivers, this is Mr. Xu," Loren said. "He's a councilman for the Gongyi province. He's hoping to get a historical designation from SACH so that they don't build on his ancestral land."

Mr. Xu put out his hand to me. It was as gnarled as tree bark. His hair and even his eyebrows were snow white, but his eyes were sharp. I took his hand in mine gingerly, as I would an ancient piece of parchment.

A tingling feeling crawled up my arm. I wanted to pull my hand back. But when I studied the old man's face, he looked entirely harmless. I wondered if he was a descendant of the men who routinely attacked me. If he was, we had obviously never met. He was alive, for one. He was old, for two. And, three, he was smiling at me without holding a sharp, pointed object over me.

No, this man was not ninja material. I relaxed marginally as I took my hand back from him. But he held on, his grip surprisingly strong for someone so old. He rubbed his rough thumb over the bones of my wrist.

"Well done, Ms. Van Alst," the old man said. "You've brought her to me as promised."

I gave my hand a yank, and it came free. Then I turned to Loren.

"I met Mr. Xu when I was in the Gongyi," she said, not appearing to have noticed anything out of the ordinary.

"You were on sacred lands without permission, it would seem." But Mr. Xu chuckled and then coughed. His entire body shook with effort. After a moment, he straightened and smiled at me.

His eyes raked over me in a proprietary fashion that made me uncomfortable. There had been younger, stronger, more powerful men to look at me in that fashion. But none of them had made me squirm. I fidgeted with the hem of my skirt, tugging it down lower on my thigh.

"Am I to believe that the IAC sent you here to see the site in Gongyi?" Xu asked, hope filling his voice. "Are they finally taking up our petition to have our homeland designated a protected historical site?"

I looked between him and Loren. Loren raised

her eyebrows at me, as though urging me to spin a tale. But she knew I wasn't here on IAC business.

"I'm here on my own," I said. "I'm doing a preliminary assessment. Can you allow me passage onto the land where Ms. Van Alst found the artifact of interest?"

"I'm afraid I don't have that power anymore, Dr. Rivers. Not on my own land." He shook his head sadly. "I am a direct descendant of the Xia—one of the few."

Maybe that was why my fingers tingled at the contact. Maybe the beef between his people and Immortals was in the DNA.

"But with Mr. Mohandis's lease on much of our lands," he continued, "I feel I am a guest in my own backyard. A stranger has come to tear down what generations of my family have worked hard to build. No matter how loudly I shout, no one seems to listen. It doesn't seem right."

"No," I agreed. "It is not right."

I ignored the continued prickles at my back and directed my ire at the land-grubbing villain in this story—Tres Mohandis. He didn't care who got in the way of his precious progress. He'd mow us all down if given the chance.

"There are not many direct descendants of the

Xia who live in Gongyi. Only a few hundred or so. Our people simply disappeared from history. We believe it was a mass genocide."

The prickles turned to buzzing in my ears. "Is there any documentation of who, or what, happened to cause it?" I asked. "A flood of the river? Or a Shang army, perhaps?" I couldn't keep the hope out of my voice that some other option had been the cause of the decimation of his people, not me.

Mr. Xu shrugged. "The truth has been lost. But it looks like Ms. Van Alst has found a clue, just like in the adventure books." He chuckled and then went through another round of coughing.

"The story is there on the bones," Loren said. "I just need to get past the Mohandis security and take another look. This time with an authenticator." She turned to me. "And maybe then the government will believe me and allow us to excavate properly, just as my father wanted."

"For many generations, the Xia have been protective of our history and culture," Mr. Xu said. "Some say there is a great secret hidden within our bones. Perhaps it has come time to share our stories with the world."

"I'm glad you are finally seeing the possibilities of progress, Mr. Xu."

Loren and Mr. Xu turned at the sound of that deep voice. But it froze me in place. The cool steel of the blade against my thigh didn't stop the trembling in my fingers.

I turned to see a massive man filling the space behind me. Tall, dark, handsome, commanding—a force. I'd turned to face Tresor Mohandis.

CHAPTER ELEVEN

I knew this was Tres. Not because I felt a tickle in my throat or because I'd seen his pictures in old portraits and recent magazines. It was because I felt the power of him. Tres was old, older than I was. He radiated the same power as Aleph.

Pictures did not do Tresor Mohandis justice. I'd never had the occasion to come face to face with the man. I'd battled the legend of him for longer than I could remember.

In my mind, he was a land-grubbing ogre. In reality, he was a husky giant. He should have been swathed in reams of fabric like his desert ancestors. Instead of a sheik's traditional garb, broad shoulders filled out a tailored suit. His pectoral muscles pushed at the front of his crisp white shirt. He stood casually on powerful thighs. Sand-touched skin was stretched across a strong jaw. Thick, chestnut locks fell just above dark eyes.

"It's the past that makes progress possible," Mr. Xu was saying.

The two men faced off. It was a white-haired, hunched-back David slinging a tiny pebble at Goliath's massive chest. The pebble bounced and fell back down to the ground.

"The contracts have been signed, Mr. Xu," said the mountain of a man in a deep baritone. "This deal will greatly benefit the people of your county."

"Many of the people who live in my county are not the original Xia Dynasty, Mr. Mohandis," said Mr. Xu. "You will be helping strangers in a land not their own. Meanwhile, the voices of the people who have been tied to the land for generations, the people of the original Xia Dynasty, are being ignored."

"History says your people were a wandering tribe who lasted only a few hundred years—not a dynasty."

"History is often wrong as told by the victors, who spoil the story," Mr. Xu said. "For example, do you know the story of the River Queen? She is the one who saved my people from the flooding of the Yellow River every year. There are many who worship her still."

Tresor Mohandis arched an eyebrow at the old man. Even though that eyebrow arched up, I knew the weight of it would crush Mr. Xu, who was simply trying to protect his heritage. And I was right.

"You believe some great ancestor will stop the flooding that will happen in a matter of weeks? Where was this queen last year when there were twenty casualties in the Gongyi? How many deaths have there been in the last five years due to flooding? My company is building a dam, which will save lives and provide jobs."

"Many of the people practice the old ways. They believe the queen is destined to return to save us from the flooding. But I will admit that I've grown more practical in my old age. I believe the dam is an acceptable idea, a welcome idea, in the meantime." Mr. Xu chuckled again before the cough raked his frail body. "But building on ancient burial grounds that have remained untouched for centuries is just wrong."

"The dead don't need the space as much as the living do," Tres said.

"So you'll stop your building plans at the dam, then?" I said.

Tres's eyes turned to me, and I realized my mistake. Under his fierce gaze, I felt trapped, like a mole with its limbs entwined. His eyes sliced my skin. I felt the healed wound on my chest protest. But for some reason, I pushed on.

"Because you won't just stop at the dam, will you?" I said. "You'll build on the land. You'll pour concrete over any site of historical significance, any stone that has a story to tell. You'll cover the story with steel buildings that scrape the sky and block out the past."

"Tired of playing in the dirt, Ms. Rivers?"

"It's Dr. Rivers."

His lip curled. "I know."

My stomach unclenched and my fist balled. I made a step to advance, but Mr. Xu beat me to it.

"We understand that progress must happen, Mr. Mohandis," Mr. Xu said. "But these are our ancestral lands. There's so much that was lost, so much we don't know. Did you know that our people were the original ninjas? The Lin Kuie, they were called."

Ice ran down my back at the words.

"These great warriors of the Xia came from the forest," Mr. Xu went on, trying to sway Tres with cultural stories. Unfortunately, I knew firsthand that the man did not prefer stories. He preferred contracts.

"Forest ghosts, they were called," Mr. Xu continued in vain. "Legend says they protected a major source of power. And you want to tear down those untouched forests without even allowing anyone to go in and preserve any history that may be buried there."

"I've invested millions of dollars in your little province," Tres said. "The hotels and resorts I plan to build will open the area up to the world and make your pockets heavy. You want me to stop the progress because there may or may not be turtle shells in the forest with some ancient scratchings about ghosts and queens?"

Loren reached into her bag. Mr. Xu gripped his walking cane. I stepped forward until I was in front of them. It was a protective stance—for them, not him. He could annihilate these two humans with a flick of his forefinger. Even with his immortal strength, he'd have more to contend with if he went after me. Tres's eyes narrowed on my stance and his lip quirked up.

"There is no written proof the Xia were a dynasty," Tres said, turning his attention back to Mr.

Xu. "Your people are a collection of small tribes. Despite what *Dr*. Rivers may have told you, the government can't go about protecting every collection of people who piled two rocks on each other and called it a home from progress. I'm offering you a chance to prosper and move into the future."

"In the meantime, you'll bulldoze their culture?" I said, a little surprised to find my voice was still there. "Take a wrecking ball to their homes? Mow down their way of life?"

Tres turned those obsidian eyes back on me. The smirk on his lips answered the question. "I think you missed your calling, *Dr*. Rivers. You should be off gallivanting with artists instead of digging around in other people's business."

I clenched my teeth. Dislike burned in my gut. But before I could voice any fire, he kept going.

"Sooner or later, progress puts us all in the ground. You should know that in your profession, Dr. Rivers."

What I knew was I'd come to this battle too late. I might not be able to stop Mohandis Enterprises's brand of progress, but there might be something else I could do to save the ancient relics of the Gongyi and get the answers I needed.

"The least you could do is give us time to excavate and save the treasures of the past from the machines of your progress," I said. "We repeat the mistakes of the past if we don't remember them or allow them to be forgotten."

"Mistakes?" His voice was as hard as granite.

I took a step back even though he didn't advance. No man had ever intimidated me, but Tresor Mohandis was old. That baby face didn't fool me. Power radiated off him, along with menace. I knew he had the power to hurt me.

It was just a flicker, but I saw it. His eyes softened at my retreat—just a fraction. Instead of advancing, he put down his heel. It was a small retreat, but it felt large.

There was recognition in his eyes. He knew me. I realized this conversation was the continuation of an old argument I couldn't remember. I'd probably been happy to forget any interaction I'd had with this man in the past. I couldn't let him see that I'd forgotten. If he knew I didn't remember, it would give him an upper hand on me.

I kept my eyes on Tres, struggling to find something familiar about him, but every instinct told me to stay away, that danger lay ahead.

"I'm not against building toward a future," I said. "But I am against erasing the past."

Something sparked in his eyes. "Some people prefer to leave the past buried," he said.

We stared off for another minute. I saw the glimmer of a memory dancing in his eyes. It wasn't a struggle to keep my look blank. I had no recollections whatsoever of him.

"The festivities are about to begin," Mr. Xu announced into our stalemate. "If you'll excuse me, I need to see to my part in the events." His hunched body executed a bow, and he took off into the crowd on slow, unsteady feet.

"Enjoy the festivities, Dr. Rivers." Tres executed a bow to befit a noble of ancient times, then he walked off, too.

Loren came up behind me and let out a long exhale. I didn't jump or reach for my blade at her presence this time. I'd forgotten she was there. It was the longest I'd ever heard her be quiet. She quickly made up for her silence.

"Holy hotness on a stick," she said.

"He has a stick, all right. Right up his tight ass."

"His very, very tight ass," Loren purred, cocking her head to the side as she watched his gait.

"He's not my type," I said as I narrowed my eyes at the confident swagger in his step.

"Oh, you would so jump those bones."

I didn't respond. Instead, we both watched him, and his tight ass, until he disappeared into the crowd.

CHAPTER TWELVE

The moment Tresor Mohandis walked away from me, he was engulfed. Women shoved up against him. Men thrust their hands at him. He took it all in stride. To the women, he gave bland, noncommittal smiles. He kept his arms crossed and an openly bored expression on his face as he looked down at the men. His closed-off posture didn't deter a single soul. They kept coming at him from every angle. I was the only person who actively stayed on the opposite end of the garden from him.

Stupid people. They didn't realize he was the snake in this garden. The shiny apple he offered them would turn this paradise into a veritable hell of concrete and steel within a year.

Mr. Xu was right to fight for his lands. Though,

admittedly, he didn't go about it in the most sane, logical, or realistic way possible. No mythical river queen could match the reality of the corporation that was Mohandis Enterprises. If the papers were signed, the Gongyi would soon be washed over by a tidal wave stronger than the Yellow River could ever manage. Mohandis would wipe out any trace of the culture that had existed and make it look as bland as the expression on his face.

That was three doors shut in my face tonight. SACHs wouldn't give us a pass. Xu couldn't let us in. And now Tres had definitively locked us out.

Still, I had to find a way to get down to that land. The River Queen might be a fairy tale, but the ninjas of the Lin Kuie were very real. I knew they'd keep coming after me. I needed to figure out what had happened two millennia ago.

I looked away from where Tres was cornered and out into the middle of the garden. The festivities had begun in earnest. The performances were working their way through the Chinese dynasties from the most recent on back through time.

Currently on dynastic display was the Zhou. The Zhou Dynasty had taken power around 1045 BCE. It was one of the longest running dynasties and birthed

Daoism and Confucianism. These thought systems of austerity and morality, and an indifference to the mysteries of life, came about during the political and social upheaval caused by the infighting in the Zhou dynasty. The man behind both thought systems, which happened hundreds of years apart, taught his followers to reject the idea that some men were born superior to others. He preached that governments should rule by virtue rather than by punishment or force.

With those seeds sown, a thousand years later that same man befriended a young Mongolian chief who dreamed of ruling the world. With the patient philosopher by his side, the young Khan would come to amass an empire across Asia before his death. Bet, the philosopher, great military mind, and Immortal, always played the long game. He was currently an adviser to the President of the United States of America.

In the center of the garden, the Zhou dancers were dressed in reams of white. They moved lithely about the space, extending their willowy arms and legs as a woman crooned in a high soprano. The dancers' movements were balletic, arms forming round circles in homage to the moon. The Zhou were well known for their moon festivals, and the dancers tilted their heads up to the crescent as part of their dance.

I looked off to the far end of the party. Loren was busy being hit on by a small crowd of men. She spoke animatedly, throwing her head back in laughter. The men's eyes were glued to her shoulder straps as though willing one to snap.

No one hit on me. I took care to exhibit all the signs of non-approach. My arms were crossed over my chest. My head was down and my eyes were hooded, not offering anyone a welcoming glance. I focused on the feel of the blade at my bare thigh beneath my skirt, using its sharp point to keep me alert to any possible danger. The ninjas had never attacked me out in the open, but this was new territory for me. I didn't quite know what to expect.

The drums started again. The pounding rhythm pushed through my skin. The pulsing beat allowed my arms to fall by my sides. I rolled my head along with the resonance of the bass, looking up to see an ornate, six-person dragon leap into the center of the garden. The dragon's shaggy red beard swayed as the dancers within it moved in time to the music.

The Chinese had been some of the earliest archaeologists. They'd unearthed dinosaur bones and called them dragons. But throughout history, the very real creature evolved into one of mythology. Over the years, the rulers used the image of the great fire-breathing reptile to symbolize their own power. But, as always, the dirt didn't lie and the truth returned to the surface. One just needed to be patient, which, at the moment, I wasn't. I wanted to get down to that land and see that dragon bone for myself. I needed to know what I was warning others against.

I plopped some dim sum on my plate. Even after sniffing it, I couldn't tell the contents. I chewed at one tentatively. It scratched the back of my throat, and I coughed. When I swallowed and the tingling was still there, I knew it wasn't because of the spicy dish.

"Let's get this over with," came Tres's deep voice from behind me. It tried to shake something loose in my mind, but self-preservation wouldn't let the memory budge. "Tell me what you want, Theta."

Theta? The name tickled the corners of my mind. Grecian columns rose in my memory. The wind from the top of Mount Olympus brushed my shoulders as someone came up behind me on the mountaintop. But I refused to turn around. I knew if I did, it would give him the upper hand. So, I continued putting dim sum on my plate, trying to keep my hands from shaking.

"I don't have time to play one of your little games," he continued. "Flooding season is coming soon, and I need to get that dam built to protect—"

"The people?"

"My investment." The two words were clipped. I knew he'd said them through gritted teeth.

I turned and looked at him then. He looked down at me with disdain. It was how I'd seen older siblings look down at a younger brother or sister who wanted to tagalong with the big kids. There was no brotherly love in his dark eyes.

"I've stayed out of your way for the last millennium," he said. "This is my territory."

"Your territory?"

"You've never shown interest in China. I gave you America."

"You *gave* me America?"

His lips pressed together in a flat line as he regarded me. "Have you become a parrot in the last few hundred years?"

I sat the plate of dim sum down and crossed my arms over my chest. I wasn't sure if it was out of protection for myself or to keep from lashing out at him. It was evident we had this conversation in the past. But like all things Asian, I didn't remember the particulars.

"What's down there in the Gongyi that you want?" He moved closer, and a chill went over my shoulders. "A bronze pot? A jade blade? A damned ancient scroll filled with chicken scratch?"

I refused to take a step back. Larger men than him had tried intimidating me. They'd failed. My right heel lifted from the pavement. I ground it back down. "The Xia culture is over two thousand years old. They didn't have parchment yet."

Tres's smile was hard. It somehow made his face beautiful, even though his words were ugly. "We can barely hold a few millennia in our minds, but you want me to care about an insignificant group of humans who may or may not have thrived for a few hundred years at most?"

"No culture is insignificant," I said. "Everyone deserves a voice."

He looked like he wanted to say more, but a noise burst up into the night. It was more drumming. I'd missed the end of the Zhou performance. It appeared I'd missed the Shang Dynasty's performance entirely. Currently on display was the oldest known organized group of Chinese tribes—the Xia.

Men dressed in dark costumes tied with sashes raced across the garden from every direction. Their swords glinted under the artificial outdoor lights. Their faces were covered in hoods with only their eyes visible.

Ninjas.

In a matter of a minute, I was surrounded by twenty men with weapons aimed at me. I lifted my skirt and withdrew the blade from the holster at my thigh. Tres looked down at me as though I'd lost my mind. He grabbed my wrist and held on. I yanked, but he was stronger than me.

"Have you gone mad?" he hissed.

I opened my mouth to explain and choked. Exactly what was I going to say? That ninjas had been hunting me for over a millennium? That I didn't know exactly why, but I thought it might have something to do with a dragon bone found on the Gongyi land?

Well, yeah. That would about cover it. There was no time to say all that. The ninjas were advancing ... in the opposite direction.

I lowered my blade at their retreat. They were nowhere near me. They were fighting against one another in what looked like a choreographed dance. None of their strikes connected. Their swords flopped about as though they weren't real steel, but flimsy aluminum. And they weren't men.

Looking more closely, I saw that they were too small to be adults. They were children, boys as well as girls. I saw ponytails emerge as they removed their hoods and continued with their performance. A banner at the side proudly proclaimed the Xia Dynasty. Mr. Xu came over to us, beaming proudly.

"These are my grandchildren," he said.

"All of them?" I asked.

Xu nodded. The children favored each other like they were a dozen sets of twins. It was a little eerie and unsettling. Their movements brought them closer to me again, and a wave of nausea overwhelmed me. I took a deep breath, and the crushing wave receded. But I was still unsettled.

At the center of the group was an older girl dressed in blues. She had a crown on her head. The ninja children ran by her with streams of blue fabric.

"She represents the River Queen," interpreted Xu. "For hundreds of years, she saved the Xia from the floods."

"Hundreds?"

"It is believed that she was immortal," Xu said. "The Lin Kuie were her guard. It is said that in return for their devotion, she gave them strength and long lives. They protected her until she transitioned on to her next life. When I was a boy, my parents told me she would rise again and return to us one day."

The children surrounded the girl in blue. They punched and kicked in time to the drumming. The audience smiled and applauded. My blood turned cold.

The girl in blue turned her back and began to walk away from the ninjas in black. The fighters came together for another sequence of movements. When they pulled away, there were red ribbons being pulled out of chest pockets, as though the group that had been defeated were truly dead.

"This represents the sorrow of the people after her death," said Mr. Xu. "And the eradication of the ancient ways of the Xia culture."

The sanguinary effect delighted the audience. It brought me back to my nightmare. The dagger fell out of my hand and clattered to the ground as the harsh dream assaulted my waking hours. The children moved closer to their grandfather to receive his praise. The closer they got to me, the larger the roiling wave of wretchedness grew until it crashed down upon me.

I staggered, expecting to hit the floor. I didn't. As

my legs gave out, I landed safe inside the arms of an impenetrable mountain.

Tres caught me. He cradled me close to his chest and looked down at me, eyes full of concern. I realized I'd been wrong. His eyes weren't a hard obsidian. They were deep pools of warmth. I remembered being atop Olympus, looking down at white columns, as he came and stood before me, grinning at me, his eyes holding that same warm gaze.

And then, everything went black.

CHAPTER THIRTEEN

I was flying. My hands were outstretched. My bare feet were off the ground. I felt the wind brush across my earlobes. The sea air tickled my nostrils. It was exhilarating. I threw my head back and laughed with the joy of it.

But I lost my balance in the air. I teetered on the wind and reached out for purchase. I found it before me, holding me aloft. It was two broad shoulders attached to the hands that held me in the air. The hands brought me back down to earth. They folded me into strong arms, stronger than an impenetrable mountain.

A face came into view. Dark eyes full of warmth shone brightly. A voice as deep as the ocean, as soft as the crashing waves, whispered in my ear.

"Theta," it whispered. "Did you think I'd let you fall?"

Tilting my head up, I saw the top of a mountain. I looked around and saw white columns. I knew deep down that I was in Greece. It was the pyramid off in the distance that confused me. Still, this dream was a welcome change from the nightmare of being held down and sacrificed on an altar.

Those strong arms wrapped around me. A defined chest pressed into my back. I relaxed into the hold, safe and secure.

"I will never let you go," the deep baritone voice said.

I knew it was Tres's voice, even though it sounded happy and kind. I felt the hard line of his jaw at the tip of my ear. Then his lush lips pressed against my earlobe.

His lips softened into a smile as they whispered their promise. "I'll never let you go, Theta."

My eyes slammed open. I winced at the bright light of the new day. Out the window, I saw the smog-filled sky and the steely skyscrapers of Beijing. It was morning, a new day, and I was back in my hotel room. But I wasn't alone.

"You didn't strike me as the fainting type."

Loren Van Alst sat cross-legged at the foot of the

bed. She was out of her dress and in cream-colored silk pajamas like we were at a sleepover. I looked down and discovered I was in pajamas, too. The ones I wore were cotton and navy blue, but they weren't mine. When I was inside four walls instead of a tent, I tended to sleep in the nude.

"Who undressed me?" I asked.

Loren grinned. "Are you hoping it was Mr. Tall, Dark, and Broody?"

My eyes raised in horror at the thought.

"Not your type?" Loren quirked an eyebrow. "Perfect, because he's exactly mine. Gorgeous, rich alpha who just needs the love of a good woman to tame him."

I sat up, my tangled hair falling in my face. "You do remember that he's cock-blocking your excavation, right?"

"Yeah, but if I could get him alone for five minutes, I could so unblock his..." She winked at me. "A night with me and I'm sure I could change his mind. Hell, he might change mine."

I flopped back on the bed, brushing my unruly hair off my forehead. "You know you can't tame men. You might train them to pee in the toilet, but they'll still leave the seat up every now and then. They're wild beasts at their core."

Loren wasn't paying attention to me. She twirled a curl of her blonde hair around her fingers with an unfocused, lustful gaze. "I'll bet he's the type to tie you up and spank you in the bedroom ... or in the basement that he's converted into a sex dungeon."

"Loren?"

"Hmm?"

I waited until her gaze cleared and trained on me. It took a full moment of silence before she blinked and looked in my direction. "What happened last night?" I lay flat on the bed, immobile, but my heartbeat raced as I awaited the recap.

Loren put out both her hands in a "stop" motion, but she waved her fingers in more of a "wait for it" sign. She folded her legs under herself and leaned forward to dish like we were schoolgirls in a high school bathroom.

"You fainted, and he caught you. Just swooped you up like in a movie." She put her hand to her heart as her eyes rolled skyward. "He was all growly and wouldn't let anyone come near you. He carried you all the way here."

None of the things that made Loren's voice go high-pitched with glee caught my attention, except that last bit. "He knows where I'm staying?"

She grinned and bobbed her head rapidly. "So he could come back any minute." She turned and looked at the door, running her hands over her fitted pajama top.

I glanced over too. We both stared at it as though it would open at any moment. It didn't.

"I have a boyfriend," I said. Never had that term seemed more childish, but human laws didn't apply to us. Sickness and health, death do us part. Zane was my life partner of over five hundred years. And we had to continuously part time and time again or face death.

"Yeah, but he's in France," Loren said.

My gaze snapped to Loren's, and I sat up in the bed. "How do you know that?"

"I saw the country code on your phone when he called. You should know..." She hooked both her thumbs toward her chest and winked. "I'm very observant. I also saw the tension between you and the Broody Billionaire. Do you two have a whole love-hate, angry-sex thing going on? Tell me and I'll back off. Hoes before bros and all that."

Now I held up my hands. "I told you, he's all yours."

I rose on the legs of a fawn and padded to the bathroom. After I turned on the faucet, I splashed cool water on my face. I stared in the mirror as though I didn't recognize myself. It felt like death had punched me in the jaw and socked me in the eye. The physical evidence of the assault was the bags under my eyes and the blotchiness of my cheeks. Nothing a proper night's rest, a little makeup, and distance between me and a certain— what did Loren call him, a Broody Billionaire?— wouldn't cover.

Fainted? Nothing like that had ever happened to me. What had that man been to me? I closed my eyes, trying to grab onto the memory of my dream in Greece inside Tres's arms. But my brain wouldn't budge.

I had gone willingly into his arms in the dream, or was it a memory? I had allowed him to lift me off the ground and into the air. Snuggled into his chest as he whispered in my ear. Had we been lovers? I couldn't even imagine us as friends.

I reached for something comforting, something that made sense, but when I reached down for my blade, I came up with air. My thigh was bare.

"Looking for this?" Loren held up my dagger from the doorway. Then she tossed it to me, hilt first. "You came to a business meeting loaded for bear. We should talk about that at some point."

I caught the dagger in the air and fingered it. Instead of responding to her query, I started one of my own. "What do you know about the history of the Xia?"

Loren returned to her position on the bed, stretching out her long form and getting comfortable. "From what my father told me, the legend is that their greatest warrior, tired of seeing his people killed by the waters, went into the Yellow River to stop the floods. A cracked-in-the-head move, right? But it turned out to be ballsy. It worked. The floods receded and he came out of the water with a woman, who would become his queen."

"The River Queen?"

Loren shrugged. "Any written history is unclear. In some writings, they say queen. In others, they say she was a goddess who came from the river itself. Whoever she was, the storybooks say she went on to rule after the Xia warrior died, becoming the first and only female monarch who wasn't a consort. My father told me the Xia Dynasty worshiped their queen because she gave them great power and everlasting life. She forged an army of assassins who moved like ghosts."

"Ninjas?"

Loren tugged at her bottom lip as she glanced at

me, then the door, and then my blade in quick succession. "Unbelievable, right?"

I didn't answer.

"Anyway, there's no official record of any of this, only legend. Some stories say the queen ruled for hundreds of years with her guard protecting her."

If I hadn't already had my own selfish reasons for figuring out this mystery, I would've been hooked by that tidbit. Matriarchal societies were a passion of mine. I wanted to know more about this unwritten queen. And I hoped, to all that was good in the world, that she hadn't been me.

"But no one would believe stories about flying ninjas," Loren continued. "And China isn't known for its female rulers. That's another reason no one believed my father and his findings on the Xia."

"They didn't believe him because he faked his findings."

"He faked one artifact." Loren's tone was clipped. "But he found that site. He told me where to go before he died, and it was exactly where he said it was."

The site and the bone might be real, but the story had holes. If I had been this River Queen, I would've never promised humans eternal life. I had no way to deliver it. My powers were not transferrable. Maybe that was why these men were after me? Because I didn't keep my promise? But no, they had enhanced powers. They got them from somewhere.

"We're leaving for the Gongyi in the morning," I said, pushing off the wall and coming back to the bed.

"We can't," Loren said. "Trains only run to Gongyi on Wednesdays. And even so, we won't get past Mohandis's security, especially not after my little performance down there the last time."

"But you've done it before. You've gotten past their security?"

The smile that spread across her face was full of wicked delight. "Why, Dr. Rivers, are you suggesting a little tomb-raider adventure?"

I sighed, but I didn't see any other way. We'd have to steal onto the land and possibly steal the evidence we needed. The answers were more important than getting permission. Before I could confirm my temporary foray into the dark side of archaeology, there was a knock at the door. I gripped the hilt and flipped the dagger blade up.

Loren shook her head and hopped off the bed. "Tetchy, tetchy." She sauntered over to the door and peered through the peephole. "Who is it?"

"Room service," called the voice.

Loren turned back to me, brow raised to ask permission. I lowered the dagger and placed it behind my back.

Loren pulled the door open and was greeted with a bouquet of flowers and a tray of food.

"Compliments of Mr. Mohandis," said the wait staff.

I moved cautiously toward the door, ignoring the flowers and focusing on the dish.

"Looks like somebody's got an admirer," Loren said.

"He doesn't admire me," I said, picking up the dish of stir-fried chicken stewed in pomegranate seeds. "We're diametrically opposed to one another."

"Sounds kinky." Loren took the bouquet, which was bigger than her head, and sat it on the dresser.

I took a bite of the dish and tried to stop the melting of my knees. It was delectable. But just because he knew pomegranates were my favorite food didn't mean Tresor Mohandis knew me.

"If you work on him," Loren said, "we wouldn't need SACH. He could give us passage onto his construction site."

"I'm not working on that beast of a man," I said around the spoon in my mouth.

"I'll let you think about that," she said as she slipped on a pair of shoes.

Suddenly, being alone sounded like the worst idea in the world. "You're not hungry?"

Loren paused and focused on my dish. "You don't look like you're willing to share."

I shrugged. "You can order something else."

She slipped off her shoes, flopped back onto the bed, and grabbed the room-service menu.

"You could've told me we didn't have a meeting with SACH before the party," I said.

She cocked her head at me. "I've learned that sometimes you have to hide the truth until people are ready to see it."

Hairs stood up on the back of my neck at her words. It felt like something I'd heard before. It felt like an omen awaiting its calendar date.

"Besides, you're still not sure whether you like me," she said. "Which is odd. Everyone likes me. I'm delightful."

"You're a pain."

"Which is how you learn that there's pleasure." She grinned and reached for the hotel phone.

We made slow progress through the street market. Vendors shoved colorful silks, plastic gems, and newly made vintage handbags in my face. Nothing had a price tag. Instead, numbers were shouted out as an opening bid for bargaining.

I didn't shout back. Didn't even open my mouth. But my eyes did catch on a sweet Tory Burch handbag. The enterprising saleslady stepped in my path and uttered a price that had me reaching for the wad of Yuan tucked inside my pocket.

In the end, I shook my head and continued, leaving the market and the bag behind. We were on a mission and had reached our destination. I stepped onto the pier behind Loren. She motioned with her hand for me to stay back. I did as she wished as she boarded a houseboat and knocked on the door.

The smell of fish permeated the air. The heel of my boot squished into something that I hoped had already been dead. I didn't look down to confirm.

I did look over my shoulder as I had been doing for the last hour. But no one was there. I'd had an eerie feeling all day that I was being followed, but no men in black flew off any buildings with blades swinging.

Loren stood in the doorway, arguing with the boat's captain. She'd said she knew another way to get down to the Gongyi. Looking at the shirtless captain whose tanned muscles rippled with tension as he glared at Loren, I realized the way she said *knew* was in the biblical sense.

Loren hitched one hip as she tried to convince the captain to give us a lift down the Yellow Sea to the Gongyi province. She'd come armed with a push-up bra beneath a low tank top. But for the second former lover in a row, the tactic wasn't working.

The door slammed in her face, and Loren stumbled back. "Asshole," she shouted to the doorframe. "Now I remember why I broke up with him."

Mohandis Enterprises was breaking ground on the site in the Gongyi in a matter of days. We could take the train into the province, but it wouldn't leave for three days, giving us even less time to sneak past the security Tres had set up around his new possession. Since it was evident we weren't going to get free access to the Mohandis-occupied lands in the Gongyi, we were opting to go by water. We just needed a vessel and a crew. Unfortunately, we were being cock-blocked at every turn.

"Did you sleep your way through Asia?" I asked Loren as she stormed down the pier.

She threw me a glare over her shoulder. "Are you slut-shaming me? What's your number?"

That shut me up. Though I'd been faithful to Zane for the last half millennium, the number of men I went through during the Renaissance period alone would put modern-day athletes to shame.

I coughed.

"Are you coming down with something?"

"No, just an allergy." I looked around but didn't see a dark, brooding billionaire anywhere. The reaction was likely the residual effects of being near two of the oldest Immortals in the same week.

"They say the flood is coming soon," Loren said as we came to the end of the pier. "No one is willing to go down once the water rises."

"We could get a boat and sail it ourselves," I mused.

Loren looked at me as though I'd gone mad. "Sure, if we had a death wish. We don't know those waters and could get lost at sea if we don't captain it right."

I'd survived at sea more times than I can remember. She could die, but I wouldn't. Which would be a shame.

I hated to admit it, but Loren Van Alst was growing on me and I didn't want to see her harmed —much. Plus, I needed her to guide me to where she'd found the dragon bone. So we'd have to stick together, and we'd have to find a way down to that land. But no matter what path we wound up choosing, it would be perilous.

"Loren, why are you doing this? Why are you trying to get back to this site? It's dangerous, and that bone probably won't make you any money. There's not much value in an ancient Chinese tribe that no one believes was a dynasty."

Loren tugged at her top lip with her teeth. She assessed me with those crystal-blue eyes. But this time, there was a crack in her gaze, like a tiny window had opened. I saw the light of truth let one ray through.

"There are some things worth more than money," she said. Then she blinked. The window shut, and she stumbled dramatically. "I can't believe I just said that."

I grinned at her theatrics. I also believed her. I knew this was about more than money. This was about her dad and his vindication. Dr. Van Alst had passed away in obscurity. Most of his earlier finds had come under scrutiny after the dragon bone he'd claimed to have found had been proven a fake.

Loren looked away from me, off into the horizon, as she continued. "If I can get that bone, the real bone, out into the light of day, and you authenticate it, it will prove my dad wasn't lying. That's worth a little danger." She turned to me, a quizzical eyebrow raised. "Why are *you* doing this?"

Same reason—to clear my name. Or maybe to implicate myself in mass genocide. Whichever answer it wound up being, I needed to know. But I couldn't tell Loren that. I went with my standard: "Every story deserves to be told."

She looked at me again. Her eyes were mirrors of

skepticism, as though she didn't believe me. Smart girl.

We walked along the shops of the pier. The wind from the waters kicked up a few strands of my hair. I looked over my shoulder again but saw no one. Then a shop proclaiming it was an apothecary that sold dragon bone elixirs caught my eye.

"Loren, I'm just gonna pop in here for a bit."

She wrinkled her nose at the sign above the shop. "Fine, I'm going to take in some actual shopping. Drinks later?"

I nodded, and she turned with a finger wave.

I entered the apothecary. The walls were lined with shelves and cases that would've been at home in a library, except from the floor to the ceiling were glass jars of every shape, size, and color. Liquids, solids, sands, and plants filled each jar. I couldn't determine a rhyme or reason to the order.

At one corner of the shop was a glass display case. Inside were bones—turtle shells, ox scapula, skulls, and femurs. They all had man-made etchings on them. The writings told of prophecies and pasts, predictions and tragedies. Dragon bones.

"Are you looking for a tincture for your health?"

I looked up at the old man who approached. He looked like he'd stepped out of a watercolor painting or an old martial arts film. His hair was all white and tied back from his face. His white beard angled down into a triangle that touched the waistband of his pants.

"The practice of drinking dragon bones is an ancient Chinese remedy," the apothecary said as he picked up a vial filled with pulverized bone.

I took a step back from the counter. My fingers recoiled, squeezing into my palms. "People ingest that?"

The old man nodded as he poured a measure of the bone powder into a teacup. "For centuries, the bones have been used to cure diseases of the heart, liver, and kidneys."

He turned his back and reached for a teakettle. It was a plastic one that was plugged into the wall using electricity to heat it instead of the fire from a stovetop.

"It is also used as a sedative to calm the mind and reduce stress and other mental ailments." He took a sip of the steaming brew. His eyes closed and his face relaxed. "Many profess the tincture staves off aging, but I believe that is because the bones are naturally high in calcium, potassium, and sodium."

He offered me a secretive smile and a chuckle, but I couldn't return either. I stared into the cup at the white flecks swirling around. "Where do you get the dragon bones?"

"There are many unearthed from the Shang Dynasty. The practice was widely popular during those times, and the bones are plentiful."

"You ever see any from the Xia people?"

The apothecary frowned. "A time or two, but they are rare. The Xia weren't a very large culture and didn't survive long. It is believed that the practice of drinking the bones began with the Xia. You look unwell. Would you like a drink?" He offered me the teacup.

As I looked into the dregs, a memory shoved at the back of my mind. I saw hands etching a message into a bone. They were my hands. Water fell on the face of the bone as I signed my name. I was crying, and my hands were shaking.

In the memory, I turned and looked fearfully over my shoulder. My heart was pounding. I tried to stand, but my knees were weak. I felt darkness encroaching on me. It felt like there was no escape, but I had to get away.

I shut my eyes at the internal struggle. When I opened them, the apothecary regarded me with worry. I took one step, and then another, until I was out of the shop. Once outside, I gulped down fresh air. Slowly, my mind settled, my heart rate calmed, and my hands stopped shaking.

Out in the park, people were practicing Tai Chi. I focused on the slow movements, matching my breath to the unhurried rise and fall of their chests. Wind lifted the lapel of my shirt. The prickles started at my neck. I turned, my hand striking out before I had fully faced my opponent. I was met with an equally formidable force.

"Why are you following me?" I demanded of Tres Mohandis.

CHAPTER FIFTEEN

Tres's lip curled as he gripped my fist in the palms of his large hands. One by one, he unfurled my fingers from their clenched fist, like he was replacing the safety on a cocked gun. Once my fingers were straight, he lowered my hand, but he didn't step away. Nor did he let go of my fingers. The rough pad of his thumb brushed over my fingertips and knuckles.

"Why would I be following you?" he asked. His voice was low. He spoke slowly, enunciating each syllable. "This is my land."

That broke his little snake-charming spell. I blinked, and my head jerked back. In the distance, I caught his name on a billboard. I turned my gaze back on him, nearly spitting my words at him. "You cannot own land."

Tres quirked an eyebrow, along with one side of his mouth. "I have a piece of a tree with ink from the ground that says differently. My company built that park and the buildings on it."

I yanked my hand from his. He let me go without a fight. We stood glaring at each other. Neither of us said a word for a full minute. He broke the silence first, which pissed me off because I was just about to say something.

"I'm surprised you're still here after you've been denied your wishes."

"Are you really?" I said. "I don't give up easily. You should know that after all these years."

He looked at me quizzically, weighing my words to assess their value as though they might be precious stones encased in rocks. "No, you never give up. Not on the things you truly want."

Great, another cryptic conversation with undertones I couldn't decipher without a Rosetta Stone. Did I mention I hate riddles?

"Why do you really want access to that land?" he asked. "And don't tell me it's for some old bones. Or that nonsense you spout about every voice being heard. You always have an ulterior motive."

I struggled to keep my face blank and bland. Blinking my eyes slowly, I was careful to offer no hints in my gaze. I exhaled a light breath to hide any tension in my jaw. "You don't know me as well as you think you do."

The sharpness of his smirk nearly cracked my veneer. "I know you better than most, *Dr.* Rivers."

His dark eyes were guarded and open at the same time. There was a way in, a path through the shield he'd placed before him. Deep down, I realized I knew the way in. But I didn't dare take a step onto the playing field. I was going to lose this game. So, I decided to lay down my pieces.

I turned from Tresor Mohandis and began walking away.

It wasn't that easy. It had never been that easy when we battled with continents between us. I doubt if it had ever been that easy when we'd met face to face in the past. I picked up the pace of my retreat. But he was on my heels in less than two breaths.

He walked beside me, but he didn't speak or accidentally brush up against me. He just kept pace with me as he waited patiently. I got the feeling he wouldn't budge until he got what he wanted. I suddenly wondered exactly how many of those battles to preserve historic lands I had actually won, as opposed to how many he'd let me win.

"I want to know the history of those people," I said.

"Why?"

I knew those words wouldn't be enough to satisfy him. But I didn't have the answers to give him other than, "Their story has been lost."

"What does it have to do with you?" he asked.

I glanced over at him. His gaze was trained on me, not on the path before us. It needn't have been. People automatically got out of his way as we walked down the sidewalk. It was like there was an invisible force around his every step. A force field that claimed the land before him as his own.

"When you've lived as long as we have, you know the only true death is to be forgotten," I said. "Buried so deep that no one remembers you. Like you were erased from time."

Staring up at him, I suddenly felt dizzy. I stumbled, my head going light. Tres reached out and caught me. We stopped walking and stood facing each other between two buildings. The park was on one side of us, an alley on the other.

One of his hands went to my hip. His long fingers

spanned to the center of my back. His thumb brushed across my hip bone in a rhythmic pattern that felt familiar. His other hand cupped my cheek and tilted my head back. The thumb of that hand brushed lightly over the slight bags that hung under my eyes.

"Why are you weak?" he asked. "Who have you been around?"

"None of your business." I straightened and tried to step out from beneath his embrace, but he held me firm.

His embrace softened as he looked down at me, eyes full of concern. The fingers at my hip and cheek tensed before he released me. I was no longer in the cage of his arms. I could break free if I wanted to. Instead, I looked up into those soft, dark eyes.

"Tell me," he said. His voice was a soft plea, not a hard demand.

"Aleph," I admitted. "I went to see Aleph a couple days ago. And now you."

The side of his mouth kicked up in something that looked like relief. He looked at my mouth. His gaze raked over my lips like they were familiar to him. His thumb returned to my face and caressed my lower lip while his eyes continued to appraise the top. His dark irises flickered as though a memory played out on the other side of them. His lips parted and his nostrils flared as though he'd already taken the first kiss and was now deciding if he would go back for seconds.

His hold was gentle but proprietary at the same time. He could tilt my head back and claim me if he chose. But I could just as easily escape his grasp.

Why was I not pulling away from him?

Was it because that earthy scent of his began to whisper a long-forgotten tale to me? Or because those dark eyes were opening and shining a light on a vision I'd seen before with my own eyes? Was it because that thumb rubbing hypnotically over my lower lip knew its way around other parts of my skin?

A sharp wind whizzed past my ear, breaking the spell. Tres's hand struck out and caught the throwing star before it had the chance to strike. His eyes widened as he saw the blood on his fingertips.

He turned his head in the direction from which the star had come. Those obsidian eyes flashed murder. He took off before my mind processed the whole scene.

Tres raced down the alley after a man who moved nearly as fast as he did. The alley wasn't very long. At the end of the narrow passage was a brick building. There was nowhere to go but up. And that was what the man dressed all in black did.

He reached up to the brick. His fingernails got purchase, and he pulled himself up. His vertical climb was short-lived, though.

Immortals couldn't fly, but we could jump pretty damn high. Tres leaped up into the air and grabbed the man by his shoulders. The two came crashing down. The ninja fell onto his back. Tres landed on his own two feet in a crouch.

The ninja did a flip to get himself back on his feet, landing upright in a fighting stance. Tres didn't give the man a moment to catch his breath. He was on him before he had his feet grounded under him.

Tres sent a series of devastating strikes at the man's head and torso. As the ninja attempted to block and protect his face and chest, Tres struck out his powerful legs and attacked the man's thighs. The ninja went down.

I wasn't used to being the damsel standing on the side, but there was nothing for me to do as Tres incapacitated the bad guy.

"Who are you?" Tres growled as he put his knee into the fallen man's chest.

"Bone for blood," said the man through a

bloodied mouth. He looked past Tres, his heated gaze finding me.

I shut my eyes at the three words I'd heard spat over the last millennia as men lay dying in their own blood. The only difference now was that I had a name to put to their kind—the Lin Kuie. And this time, the blood spilled was not by my hands.

I heard a crack and knew Tres had snapped the man's neck. Instead of looking for confirmation, I turned away. Tres stalked around to the front of me like an angry bull.

He held up the throwing star in his bloodied hand. "Tell me the truth, Theta."

I stared at the blood seeping through Tres's fingertips from the sharp points of the blade. "I don't know what you're talking about."

He tossed the blade aside. It clattered to the ground. He grabbed my shoulders, pressing his bloodied fingers into the shirt beneath my jacket. "He's been following you—from the docks to the shop. Why?"

I met his gaze with a defiant shake of my head. "If you know that he was following me, then that means you were following me, too."

"Enough, Theta." He gave me a shake. "Answer me."

"I don't know what they want." I reached up and broke his hold on me with my forearms. "I'm trying to find out. I think the answer is buried somewhere on that land you're about to bulldoze."

He looked at me skeptically. "If this is some ploy, like in Thebes…"

"I don't know what you're talking about," I shouted. I was tired and fed up with not having the answers to these riddles everyone kept throwing at me.

Tres stilled. Then he studied me, searching my face for … something. I held still as he gaped in disbelief.

"You don't…" He swallowed and tried again. "You couldn't have forgotten…" His lips pressed together like he was about to make the M sound, like he was about to say *me*. But he didn't. His lips parted as he took a step back.

I said nothing as he continued his retreat. His feet picked up, and he backed away from me with narrowed eyes, flared nostrils, and bared teeth.

He turned and punched the brick wall. I felt the reverberation roll through me. A hairline crack went up the side of the building. A few pieces crumbled and crashed down onto the ground. Without a second glance at me, he stormed out of the alley, leaving me alone with the dead body.

CHAPTER SIXTEEN

After the attack, I walked the city for a few hours to work off some of the adrenaline. I was also trying to jump-start my memories. But try as I might, I couldn't recall a single thing about Tres Mohandis or Thebes.

The Beijing skyline at night looked like the interior of a nightclub. The sky was a dark blue streaked with neon lights, painting electric patterns of fuchsia, aqua, peach, mint, and violet. I didn't find progress beautiful. I liked old things, ancient things. Things with a bit of dirt on their faces, scuffed at the edges. Dented up instead of brand new.

I turned away from the city lights and stared at the Jiankou Mountains in the distance. The Great Wall curved into those mountains, forging its most precipitous peak. I knew the real reason that wall had been built. My records of the actual event were back on my island. But the truth of my time in the Gongyi, the facts of my relationship with Tres Mohandis, was a dark void in my mind. No matter how bright a light I shone on things, bits and pieces of my past constantly slipped through my fingers and the cracks in my mind.

I headed back to the hotel. As I reached the entrance, I tried to figure out how to get out of drinks with Loren. Girls' night with my perceptive new sidekick was the last thing I needed in my current mental state.

I felt the tickle at the back of my throat announcing the presence of another of my kind. I turned on my heel, preparing to run. That may have been cowardly, but I didn't want to deal with him again this evening. I didn't want to face the challenge in his eye or the anger at my ignorance of our past.

It was the soft chuckle that halted my retreat. I turned back and watched his frame as he leaned against the front desk counter. He looked the same as the last time I'd seen him, but I stared at him as though it were the first.

His broad back made a rounded M shape as he hunched his tall form down to speak with the concierge. Ropey forearms rested on the glass of the counter. His shirtsleeves were rolled up to show the light smackling of dark hair on his tanned forearms. He wore jeans that showed off his toned ass.

"Your wife is a lucky woman." The female concierge batted her eyelashes at him and leaned her chest forward in an open invitation. "She'll be thrilled you flew all the way here from France just to see her."

"*Oui*, she will. *Maintenant*, if you'll just give me her room key?"

"I can't give you her key. It's against hotel policy. But I can buy you a drink while you wait for her to come back from wherever she is." The concierge continued to bat those lashes as though there were something in her eye. I wanted to tell her that move wasn't sexy at all, but I felt no need.

Zane frowned. Well, pouted was more like it. I could see the concierge buckling under his lush lips. Poor woman—she was no match for him. Before Zane could launch the final assault, his nose twitched. His smile widened. The concierge leaned in, ready to take her shot, but he turned away from her.

His gaze started at the floor. He took in my hiking boots and worked his way up until he was looking at my face. I was in his arms by the time he met my gaze.

"Never mind," he told the concierge. "I have found a way in."

I ignored the woman's glare as I buried my nose in Zane's neck. Inhaling deeply, I got a hit of the earthy smell of sage, the buttery smell of croissants, and the tart smell of acetone. His arms wrapped around me, lifting my feet off the floor until he had my whole being in his embrace.

"You're here," I said.

"Happy anniversary, *mon coeur*."

I pulled away from him, but not so far I couldn't run my fingers through his thick locks. Brushing back the handful of unruly hairs that constantly fell into his hooded eyes, I said, "But you had a showing. Your first in decades—"

He kissed the fleshy blade of my hand, then nosed at my wrist until his lips met the center of my palm. Raising his face upward, he scaled over the top of my knuckles and kissed each of my fingertips one by one.

"It always makes me appear more mysterious when I don't show up," he said. "And it makes the sales prices on the pieces go higher."

I wanted to protest. That showing had been

important to him. I knew how much he'd been looking forward to receiving praise for his work in this day and age. But his joy-filled smile took my breath, and he took advantage. He lowered my body and brought my lips to his. His kiss silenced any more conscious thought.

I didn't remember how we got to my room. I only remember my lips against his. My tongue danced a practiced duet alongside his. My hands wrapped around his neck, tracing his spine, pressing into the flat planes of his abdomen.

His hand slipped my jacket off, and I left him for a brief second as I disentangled myself from the garment. When the jacket hit the floor with a thud, I went to wrap my arms around him again, but he held me at bay.

"What is this?" he asked. Concern etched out the passion on his face. I followed his gaze down to the shoulder of my shirt and saw the blood.

"The blood is not mine." I went for the buttons of the shirt, pulling the ruined garment open to show him my unmarred flesh. "It's Tres's."

Myriad expressions and emotions crossed Zane's face, many of which I couldn't ever remember seeing before. "He's here?"

I nodded.

Zane raised an eyebrow. "Alive?"

I frowned at the hope in his voice. "I didn't kill him, if that's what you mean."

Zane's face fell in disappointment. But then it transformed into something dark, something I'd never seen before. "Did he hurt you?"

I crossed my arms over my chest. "No, it was a … misunderstanding. I … We…"

Zane waited. His expressive face had gone blank. Another look I'd never seen. I decided I didn't like it and wanted it to go away.

"It's a long story," I finally said. "Can we talk about it later? I would much rather be naked with you."

Tension melted off Zane's shoulders. His lips curled up in the way they did before I found myself flat on my back with him looming over me. "You want to be naked?"

"Yes, please. And ravaged."

His grin spread as he set about his two tasks. I was naked in no time flat, then tossed onto the bed on my back. Zane knelt before me as he often did when I came to him nude. I was aching between my thighs as he took his time taking off his shirt. My nipples were hard points as he unbuckled and lowered his jeans.

"I remember the first time I saw you," he said as he bent over me, dipping his head to nip at my shoulder. "Knee-deep in the sands of Giza."

I was already punch-drunk on his brand of foreplay, but his words brought me back to sobriety. "Egypt? We met in Rome in the fifteenth century. We didn't go to Egypt together until two hundred years ago."

Zane blinked up at me. His gaze looked lost and unfocused. The wayward locks fell low on his forehead as his brow crinkled. And then he grinned. "Of course. My mind is hazy with want."

He leaned down to capture my lips, but I sat up in the bed, giving him a push. "Or you forgot."

Zane straightened his arms, caging me in. He took my face in his hands. "What is this?" He wiped at the tear that rolled down my cheek.

"What if you're losing some of your memories of me? What if one day you forget me entirely?"

"Not possible," Zane said.

"Yes, it is." In my mind, I saw Tres's face when he realized I didn't remember him from Thebes or our time before.

"Not for me." There was a note of sadness in Zane's voice, but by the time I blinked, it was gone. Back was the tilted smile he wore every day we were together. Back was the mischief in his hooded eyes. "I remember every detail of you, *mon coeur*. I put them all in my art."

He coaxed me back down to the bed, and I followed his command. I was a lamb, and he was my shepherd. I would follow him anywhere.

"We shed our memories because we no longer need them to survive. We only keep what we need."

Zane delivered feather-light kisses along my brow. It felt less like a seduction and more like a benediction. His every utterance against my skin was a blessing.

"You are as necessary to me as breathing, *mon coeur*. You are my True North, *ma petite nova*."

He captured my lips, and his tongue stroked mine in a repetitive chant. His hands caressed my flesh as though seeking salvation. His fingers entwined with mine and we gripped each other down to the webbing, joining our hands together in a prayer of devotion, but not to any god, only to each other.

"Even if I forgot a single second, I would always gravitate back to you. This isn't love, Nova. I worship you, you know that."

His fingertips traced a path from my right breast and then crossed to my left. Zane's knees parted my thighs. He gazed down at the treasure he found there. His sigh was one of veneration. He whispered something in ancient Gallic. It sounded like an invocation, a summoning of a deity. I writhed beneath him with eagerness for more of his touch. The only words of the ancient prayer I caught were the ones meaning *cherish* and *honor*.

I reached up and pulled him down to me, undulating with impatience as he continued his adulation. His hard cock found my entrance, guided by blind faith. We lay prostrate, our bodies rocking together, reaching for the bliss we knew we would achieve if we remained devout in our practice of reverence for each other.

The glory of our coupling gripped me hard. My climax stole my breath and shook my body down with a mighty vengeance that, if I hadn't already been on my back, would've brought me to my knees. As I came back down to this plane of existence, Zane breathed into my hair and whispered, "Amen."

CHAPTER SEVENTEEN

The *scratch scratch* of pencil on parchment woke me. Zane sat in the hotel room's solitary office chair with his bare feet kicked up on the bed. A sketchpad was in his lap, his pencil sailing across the paper.

"Don't move, *ma petite nova,*" he whispered. "The afternoon light is casting the perfect amount of illumination on your flawless cheekbones."

I inhaled and let out a soft sigh at his tone of reverence. Under the cover, my toes curled as the lead in his pencil continued to play my favorite tune. My inner thighs felt a slight twinge at the rigors we'd been through last night. And then, finally, my mind processed the words he'd said.

I sat bolt upright in the bed. "Afternoon?"

"Ah." He groaned. His pencil halted and scratched the paper like the needle on a record player. "You moved."

"I slept through the morning?" The sheet fell from my torso, and the day's light warmed my bare breasts. I stared out the window to see the sun high in the sky.

"Well, you did say ravage." Zane's voice was anything but apologetic. He picked up his pencil again, making long strokes on the paper. "I must not have done it properly if you are up and about."

"I can't lie around all day." I swung my legs out of the bed, and my bare feet hit the cold floor. "I'm working."

Zane paused in his sketching to watch my naked body as I hopped from foot to foot. I knew he was admiring his handiwork—the love bites and fingerprints he'd left on my skin from our amorous activities. They were faint and would fade in an hour or so, unless he got me back into his clutches.

He tapped the top of the pencil against his full bottom lip. There was no eraser there. Zane never erased his work. Instead, he covered his mistakes with something more beautiful.

The way he was looking at the patterns he'd left on my skin told me he had new designs in mind. For a second, I held still for him. I let him look his fill and decide how he would contort me, mold me, shape me. But then, as his gaze hooded and his vision clouded in that way it did when he had a spark of inspiration, I shook my head and backed away from him. I heard him chuckling as I turned and made a mad dash into the bathroom.

As I said before, Zane was meticulous and methodical when it came to his art. If I allowed him, he'd have me in the bed all day and into the night. I paused, looking in the mirror at my tousled hair, bee-stung lips, and dilated pupils.

Why was staying in bed with him all day a bad idea?

"You still intend on going to the Gongyi?" he called from the other room.

Oh, right. The ninjas, genocide, and a historical site that was about to be bulldozed by a villainous land-grabber. Any other time, a weekend in bed with Zane would have been the best idea in the world. But right now, I had to keep my wits and focus. I was on a time-sensitive mission.

"I am," I said, pulling out a pair of jeans from my travel bag and stepping into them. Then I reached in and grabbed a shirt.

"Even though Tres won't allow you passage?"

"Like that's going to stop me." I gathered my hair in one palm and pulled the strands through a band. "I'll just find another way."

"That's my girl."

I leaned my head out of the bathroom. Zane was looking down at the drawing in his lap. His gaze was pensive. His voice hadn't sounded proud; it sounded resolved.

"You're disappointed that I'm missing our time together?" I asked. "This won't take long. Two weeks tops, and then we can go to the villa or wherever you want."

He looked up. As his gaze left his rendering of me and found the live me, he smiled. The expression didn't reach his eyes. Before he could respond, there was a knock at the door. A pounding, actually.

"Nia, you slut. Who do you have in there? Is it Mr. Tall, Dark, and Broody real estate investor?"

Zane turned from the door with raised eyebrows. I gave him a look that said *you know better*. From the first time I saw Zane in the streets of Rome, I lost all interest in other men. It had taken decades for him to get me in bed. Sometimes I wondered if the chase then, and the anticipation of when I'd see him next in this time, was just as good as our actual lovemaking. No other lover I'd ever had could do what Zane did to my body, to my heart, to my mind. He had me, and he knew it.

"Let me guess?" he said. "Ms. Van Alst?"

I nodded. "The woman's a menace. She won't go away. Just go and put something on—"

Zane was already up and out of his seat. I noted the marking of the ancient number seven on his back as he went to the door. I watched his firm buttocks rise and fall as he padded over on bare feet. Zane had no problems with nudity. He opened the door, and Loren got an eyeful.

"Hel"—her eyes dipped down—"lo."

"Ms. Van Alst." Zane extended his hand.

Loren was looking low. Luckily, her hand met its mark and not where her gaze was fixed. "You must be the French boyfriend."

"Boyfriend?" Zane raised his eyebrows, giving Loren the full glow of his hazel eyes. "Dr. Rivers and I are far more than friends. She is my muse, my subject of idol worship."

That silenced Loren, whose mouth worked like a fish out of water trying to find a response.

"Do come in, Ms. Van Alst." Zane stepped back from the door, sweeping his arm across the expanse of the tiny hotel room with all the flourish of a French aristocrat.

I tossed him a robe. Zane didn't bother going into the bathroom to cover modesty he didn't possess. He gave us his back and slid into the robe. Loren gave me a wide-eyed, double thumbs-up behind his back.

"I was coming by for lunch since you stood me up for drinks ... and breakfast," Loren said when Zane faced us again. "Now I see why, and I can't be mad."

"Lunch sounds lovely," Zane said, coming to stand beside me. He bussed my temple with a wicked grin. "I'm famished."

"Why don't you get dressed and we'll all go out?" I said.

"Or you could stay comfortable in what God blessed you with, and we could stay in," Loren offered, her eyes on Zane.

Zane gave Loren the same grin he'd given the concierge last night—the one that said *you're welcome to look, but there will be no touching*. Then he disappeared into the bathroom after I shoved him in with his bag. I heard his deep chuckle from behind the door. Incorrigible man.

"I didn't know they made them like that in France," Loren said.

Zane wasn't exactly French, but, like most

Immortals, he had a preference of region. He'd been born before the formation of Gaul, which would later become France. He shared the people's Mediterranean features, dietary preferences, work ethic, and liberal views. So, he preferred to make his home in that region of the world.

I, on the other hand, didn't have a regional preference. I shared the features of a few races and ethnicities. I ate whatever was put in front of me. I worked just as hard as I played—although not so much lately. And I went wherever history called me.

"Listen," Loren said. "I may have found us a way down to the Gongyi, plus a way to bypass the security once we get there."

I tilted my head as I regarded her. "Is it legal?"

Loren bristled. "Why would you assume..."

I tilted my head to the other side and raised my eyebrows even higher.

Loren sighed and rolled her eyes. But before she could respond, the bathroom doorknob turned.

"Let's talk about it later," I said as Zane came out in jeans and a linen shirt. He looked rumpled, but it worked for him.

We left the room with Loren querying Zane about his dietary preferences. Like me, Zane would eat anything that was put in front of him. So we decided to head to the market district to see what the fresh catch of the day was.

As we came down the stairs, I felt dizzy and lost my footing. Zane reached out a hand and brought me into his side. His gaze filled with concern as it searched mine. Then the concern cleared. It was replaced by something dark and stormy. His body stiffened as he turned.

I looked past Zane to see Tres Mohandis leaning casually against the front desk. His careless gaze hardened when he saw Zane.

Zane was not a possessive man. We spent weeks, months, at one point even years, apart. But he never doubted my devotion to him, and I never doubted his. Which was why the feel of his fingertips digging possessively into my hip was a bit of a shock.

We made our way down to the front desk and came face to face. Loren, Zane, and I stood in a semi-circle surrounding Tres. For a full moment, we just stared at one another. It was something out of an old Hollywood Western at high noon. Tres looked to Zane and then me. I looked between Tres and Zane. Loren mostly looked at Tres.

"Mr. Mohandis." Zane broke the standoff, sticking out his hand in either a welcome or a truce. I wasn't sure.

Tres stared at Zane's outstretched hand for a full breath, examining it as though looking for the trick. And then, finally, when I thought he would refuse, Tres took Zane's hand. It was my imagination that thunder crackled above at the contact.

"I assume we've met before," Tres said. "You'll forgive me if I've forgotten your current name."

Zane's tone was placating, but his smile was fake. "No need to try to recall it. I'm sure a man like you would forget it after a second."

A rumble of assent sounded deep in Tres's throat.

"What are you doing here?" I asked Tres, taking a step between the two men. I was certain the humans present could feel the power radiating off them. I certainly could.

Tres turned those dark eyes on me. Unlike yesterday, they were completely shuttered. Not an ounce of light escaped their depths. His voice, when he spoke, was passionless and matter-of-fact. "I came to check on you after your incident the other day."

"Yes," Zane said. "I heard she wounded you during some misunderstanding?"

Loren turned to me and blinked rapidly. Her lips crooked in a proud grin. But at least this time she didn't give me the thumbs-up.

Tres lowered his chin to glare down at me. His jaw was a hard line. His eyes narrowed to dark slits.

I held my breath. Zane and I had never gotten around to having an actual conversation about what had transpired between Tres and me. He didn't know there was a third party—a dead ninja—in the mix. I didn't want him to find out now, especially not like this. Not with an Immortal, who Zane clearly had a history with, lording it over his head that he knew something about the woman he loved that Zane didn't.

And so I held my breath, hoping the fact we were out in public with a human woman standing in our midst would deter Tres from revealing too much. What he wound up saying shocked me more than any other revelation could.

"I came to offer Dr. Rivers passage onto the site in the Gongyi," Tres said.

I blinked, running his words through my mind. Tres smirked, knowing he'd caught me off guard and relishing in my imbalance.

"You and Ms. Van Alst have my permission to access the site and the untouched lands where you claim there is something of historical significance."

Tres looked at me pointedly. I knew he was referencing my words from the encounter yesterday.

He was giving me leave to find out why those ninjas were after me. I wanted to say thank you, but my lips wouldn't work.

"That's very fine of you, Mr. Mohandis," Loren said. "You should let us thank you properly. We were just heading out to lunch. Would you care to join us?"

"No." Tres barely glanced at her. "I'll be leaving this evening. I have business to attend to while you two go play in the dirt," he said to me. Then he turned to Zane and added, "And you go play with your finger paints."

And, with that, he marched out the door.

CHAPTER EIGHTEEN

Before the drinks were served, Zane had completely charmed Loren. The two became lost in a discussion about some obscure Dutch artist, and I tuned out of the conversation.

I was antsy, looking over my shoulder at every turn. I didn't feel any hairs creeping up my neck to indicate I was being followed. Instead, I felt Zane's long fingers grazing the space between my hairline and shoulder blades. Even though I felt the beginnings of fatigue from the impact of being around not one, not two, but three Immortals in the past week, I still felt strong as I relaxed in his casual embrace.

"Forgers get a bad rep, but it takes a lot of

technique to replicate someone else's art," Loren was saying. "In a way, forgery is an art in its own right."

"I agree with you." Zane stroked his long fingers into my hair with his fingertips and then kneaded my neck with his thumb.

Loren, who had puffed herself up in anticipation of an argument, paused and stared at him. Then she leaned in as though she thought she'd found a fellow fox in the hen house. "Did you know that Michelangelo launched his career by passing off a replica of the *Sleeping Eros* as an original?"

Loren didn't wait for Zane to acknowledge that he did indeed know that fact. And the reason Zane knew it was because he had been the one to teach the young artist how to make the copy.

"Michelangelo sold the sculpture to a cardinal who was a relation to the Pope," Loren continued. "Today, that would be like selling to the nephew of the king or president, the highest officer in the land. And when the cardinal found out it was a fraud, did he get pissed? No, he was impressed by the quality of Michelangelo's work."

"I know," Zane said, nodding. "Cardinal Raffaele Riario even hired Michelangelo to do more work— his own original work this time. The cardinal became his first patron."

"Too bad there are no cardinals like him nowadays." Loren huffed and took a sip of her wine.

Zane winced. I hadn't met this Riario, but by Zane's wince, I assumed the cardinal's reputation hadn't been all glowing.

"In the Renaissance," he said, "apprentices in the arts learned by copying the works of the masters. Their mentors knew they had become artists in their own right when the mentor couldn't tell the difference between the master's work and the student's."

"Like a final exam?" said Loren.

"Exactly." Zane nodded.

"So, mimicry is a sign of ability." Loren leaned back in her chair, looking smug.

Zane gave a slight shake of his head. "Mimicry is an art, but the crime is in the lie of passing off the work as authentic."

Instead of responding, Loren shrugged and took another sip of her wine. Zane chuckled and grabbed the check. He bussed me on my temple, then stood and disappeared inside the cafe to pay the bill. Loren scoped out his backside as he passed her by. I narrowed my eyes at her brazenness.

"Don't worry," she said when she caught my gaze. "I'm just looking. He's not my type." Loren frowned and cocked her head, still openly studying Zane. "Too perfect."

"You say that like it's a bad thing."

"I like a bad boy who I know I have to keep my eye on. Zane seems like one of the good guys. You know, trustworthy." She wrinkled her nose. "Those men give me anxiety. You never expect them to do anything wrong, and then inevitably they do."

I looked at Zane. He leaned against the counter, chatting up the barista who counted out his change. The barista counted slowly, obviously trying to keep Zane engaged in the conversation. But like always, Zane's gaze found mine. That tilt-a-whirl smile canted even more. Those hooded eyes opened wider, showing me everything. I was the one hiding an entire world of secrets inside.

"In my life, I've found that when something or someone is too good to be true," Loren said, "it's usually because they are."

Her words were said casually, but her gaze on Zane's backside was appreciative. She shrugged and turned back to me, staring at me for a moment. Pulling her lower lip into her mouth, she tugged at the top of her dress. She tugged it in the wrong direction—up instead of down.

"But like I said," she said, smoothing out her

skirt, "I'm not going to try and steal him away from you or anything."

My shoulders jerked, and I sat erect in my chair. "It's not like you could."

"Well, I'm not going to try," she said firmly, and then her mouth twisted. "I know girls don't take kindly to that."

"No, Loren, they don't."

She crossed her arms over her covered chest. "I grew up with a single dad who was a cultural anthropologist who studied polygamous peoples and communal living. So, some of my social education is askew. You have to admit, in the animal kingdom, monogamy is a strange and infrequently observed practice."

I stared at her before bursting out laughing. "Well, I thank you for your consideration."

She shrugged. "What are friends for."

"Is that a question?" I chided.

"No," she said after a moment of consideration. "I think I've got the basics down now."

Later that night, Zane and I lay in bed. He traced swirling patterns on my bare skin. I wondered what he was drawing. I knew I only had to ask and he'd tell me.

"What's between you and Tres?" I asked instead.

He huffed a small laugh. His breath was hot on my skin, but his words were cool. "Gimel and I have never seen eye to eye." Zane used Tres's Aramaic name. "He sees the world as something to conquer and tame. I prefer to look for the beauty in the natural state of things." His fingers spanned my back and gave a squeeze, then he began tracing the swirling patterns again.

"There was a coldness between the two of you."

"We have lived a very long time, Nova. We've all seen one another at our best and at our worst."

"Has Tres ever been at his best?"

Zane left his pattern-making and lay down alongside me. "It would take too long for me to dig through my memories to find an example."

I pressed myself up on my side. Splaying my hand over his heart, I looked into his smoldering eyes. "Zane?"

"*Oui, mon coeur?*" He dipped his head and nudged at my hand on his chest until I gave him my fingertips to kiss.

"Have you ever forgotten someone?"

"I have forgotten a lot of people." He ducked his

head until my palm pressed into his temple, rubbing his face against my hand like a large cat seeking attention.

"No," I said as I acquiesced to his demands and ran my fingers through his hair. "Have you ever forgotten one of us? Another Immortal?"

He reached up and wound his fingers in my hair before he pulled me in for a kiss. When we parted, he peered into my eyes. "Ask me what you really want to know, Nova."

I'd known about Zane for over a thousand years, even though we hadn't met face to face until about five hundred years ago. It was surprisingly easy to avoid other Immortals if you tried. I had no recollection of encounters with Tres during the time we may have shared in Greece, or any other time before that. But, apparently, an encounter had happened.

"I think Tres and I knew each other in the past," I said. "But I can't remember him."

It felt beyond awkward asking the man I loved if he knew if I'd had a relationship with a man he clearly didn't like, a man I clearly didn't like. If there had been something between Tres and me millennia ago, it obviously wasn't worth remembering.

"He has animosity toward me now," I said. "I don't know what I did to him."

"You likely rebuffed him. He's the type who's used to getting what he wants. But that is not what's truly bothering you, is it?"

My heartbeat quickened as Zane rolled me onto my back. He ran a gentle hand along my throat, and I felt breathless. When he planted a soft kiss at the edge of my lips, my mouth went dry, damming up the words inside.

"When are you going to tell me what's really bothering you?" he asked. "The real reason you're here in China."

I swallowed, but my throat was thick. I had to force the words out. "The bones?"

"No, the Lin Kuie."

I took in a sharp breath. The tips of my fingers, where I held onto his biceps, tingled. "I never said that name to you."

"No," he agreed. "Not while you were awake. But you've said it many times in your sleep. You've had nightmares for hundreds of years."

My hands fell away from his biceps. I folded them at my chest and looked away from the man I swore I knew better than anyone in the world. "You've never said anything."

Zane took my chin in his thumb and forefinger and turned me back to face him. "Neither have you. We spend more time apart than we do together. There are bound to be things we prefer to keep to ourselves. But now you're here in China."

I swallowed again, not knowing why it was so hard to tell him this. Zane loved me—no. He worshiped me. He wouldn't think any less of me. "I think I may have done something in the past."

"What something?"

"I don't know. I'm trying to find out."

He studied me for a moment, regarding me through a lens of time that only an Immortal could see through. "We've all done things in our past," he said. "Many things that we're not proud of. But that doesn't make us who we are. We are not the sum total of our past. Not with how often the wind has shifted over our lifetimes."

I sat up, pulling the covers around my chest. "What if I've killed people?"

Zane sat up behind me. His strength and warmth surrounded me. He rested his chin against my shoulder. "You have killed before. We all have. For survival. As an accident. For a host of other reasons that we might want to forget."

"Doesn't make it right." I hugged my knees into my chest.

"Digging it up won't change it." Zane crossed his arms over mine, enveloping me in acceptance and love. But I still couldn't break free of the guilt and shame of the unknown.

I turned to peer into his eyes. They shone brightly with understanding and adoration. "You don't think I should go?"

He released me with a sigh, lying back against the headboard. "Two weeks of hacking through China, or two weeks where I ravage you? If you have to think about it, I'm not as good as I thought."

I looked at my lover sprawled on the bed. It wouldn't be a choice, not normally. I would jump at the chance of staying with Zane. I winced as a cramp took hold of my leg. The allergy, that humanizing effect that happened when Immortals got too close for too long, didn't normally hit me so hard and so fast. But I'd been around an Immortal every day this week, not to mention two of the oldest. And then there were the ninjas. The symptoms were compounding and rendering my body pervious to the discomforts of humanity.

When Zane saw my discomfort, he took the matter in hand. He rose and ran his fingertips down my thighs, then kneaded his knuckles at the spot that had seized. After a few moments of his care, the tension eased. I relaxed under his nursing and the unease fled my body, chased away by his skilled hands.

"You could come with me," I said.

He smiled sadly and shook his head. "You'll need your strength. My presence would only slow you down."

With the cramp now gone from my thighs, he spread them apart. His hands kneaded the creases at each of my thighs. I inhaled as his thumbs brushed the naked skin of my core once, twice. Then I moaned with need.

"Go quickly," he said, lowering himself to the mattress. His hands pressed my thighs further apart. "Find what you need and then return to me so that I may worship at the apex of your thighs."

Zane lifted his head and looked out the window at the dawning sun.

"It's a new day," he said. "Time for my morning devotions to my goddess. Amen, *mon coeur.*"

And, with that, his head disappeared at his ready-made altar. Speaking with his tongue, he began his worship.

CHAPTER NINETEEN

I left Zane lying in bed the next morning. We never said goodbye at airports or train stations. One of us always left the other in bed. That person was usually me.

I was the one often gallivanting around the globe. Zane was a homebody. He was happiest in his studio surrounded by his paints, canvases, and clay. He didn't feel the need to go out and seek answers. Didn't care to interact with the modern world or reminisce about past lives. He was content to paint and mold the world as he saw fit.

I envied him that. I was never satisfied with the status quo, and I always needed to dig deeper, ask more questions, uncover the hidden truth. And so I left him tangled in the sheets after a night of lovemaking so tender that I cried into his shoulder at my release.

He held on to me until the morning, promising he'd never let me go no matter how far I was from him. I was his True North, he repeated, and he would always gravitate back to me.

He would be flying out later this evening, back to France. He said he'd wait for me at the villa, no matter how long I took, and we'd pick up where we left off.

I had a headache and my eyes were puffy as I boarded the train out of Beijing. The headache was from the allergy, the puffy eyes were from the ache in my heart. I felt weak, but it was due more to the distance being placed between me and my lover than because of the time we spent together. It had only been three days, but multiply that by three immortals and it might as well have been a month. The fatigue had settled in.

The train ride into the Gongyi province was twelve hours long. It was long enough to get over the headache, to soothe my heartache, and restore my energy. I hated to admit it, but Zane was right. If he'd come with me, we both would've been miserable from the allergic reaction to each other.

I rested my head back on the headrest and

looked out the window at the scenery passing by, looking for any familiarity in the landscape. If I had been here two thousand years ago, much would have changed in that time.

Much of the countryside was industrialized with factories dominating old, rundown temples and squat homes. As we moved further away from the city, the air and sky got clearer, the buildings more spaced out, and the roofs lower than the horizon. At intervals, there was sometimes nothing but greenery —trees, fields, and foliage-covered mountains. But we never went for long without seeing a touch of humanity.

I pulled out the copy of the photo of the dragon bone that Loren had given me and stared at my writing. I spoke, wrote, and read every language known to man. But this was the first time I couldn't decipher my own writing.

My name at the bottom was clear as day to me. I pieced together the symbol that read Lin Kuie. But I was sure that that bit of understanding had gotten through the locks in my mind because of the guilt I felt at the center of my chest. This mystery wanted to be solved, however it wouldn't give up its clues so easily.

"Have you figured out what that says yet?"

I looked up to see Loren. She'd returned from the food car with two rice bowls and drinks. I took the bowl in one hand and looked back down at the photograph I held in my other hand.

Shaking my head, I let out a heavy sigh. My eyes squinted at the photograph in the waning light of the day. There were characters I'd etched into the bone that didn't make sense. Above the symbol for the Lin Kuie, I also picked out the symbols for sacrifice and queen. Beside that symbol were two others I couldn't place in any Chinese dialect.

"Right now, it's just a series of characters and symbols having to do with the Lin Kuie making a sacrifice to their queen." I squinted again, trying to determine if I'd wrote *to* their queen or *of* their queen. I wasn't sure which type of sacrifice would be worse.

I sat the photograph down and cupped the warm bowl of rice in my hands. Flexing my fingers around it, I tried to release some of the tension I'd gathered there from tracing the etchings in the picture. Then I picked up the chopsticks and shoveled the food into my mouth.

Loren picked up the photograph from my lap. "Lin Kuie? Isn't that also from a video game? *Mortal Kombat*? One of my exes used to play that game ad nauseam. Thought he was a real ninja because he took classes at a dojo in a shopping center."

I shrugged as I swallowed another heaping of the rice. "Many of the history books, folklore, and legends say the Lin Kuie were the first ninjas. They were basically mercenaries who worked for the upper classes. None of these men were highborn. They came from the ranks of the lower classes, trained to be secretive about their existence as well as their actions."

Loren twisted her mouth before she spoke, as though she wasn't sure of her words. "Do you think any of this was real? The queen or the … ninjas?"

I studied the scenery before I answered her. If she hung around with me, she was very likely to run into some real ninjas. I owed her something of the truth. "There's always a kernel of truth in every story told. I believe there are likely men, people, in the Gongyi who want to protect their heritage. Some may try to do it through the legal system, like Mr. Xu, while others may take a more mercenary approach."

Loren settled back in her chair beside me. She turned her body to face mine and tucked her long legs under her. "The ninja, the Lin Kuie, written about on the bone, you think they were just trying to protect the queen?"

"I'm not sure," I said, playing with the last dregs of rice in my bowl. "They were either trying to protect her ... or sacrifice her."

"So my dad was right? They had a female monarch?" Loren's grin was triumphant, but it soon fell as she thought through to the second part of what I said. "But why would they sacrifice her?"

I set the empty bowl aside and picked up the photograph again. "Same reason some tribes sacrificed animals to the gods, that Abraham was set to sacrifice his son to God, that there are coups in kingdoms, pirate ships, governments, and militaries—for power."

I looked again at the photograph. *To* or *of*? I didn't often write cryptically, especially not when I wrote down my records. I spent too much of my time deciphering old relics. But the way I'd written this could mean either a sacrifice to the queen or a sacrifice of the queen.

Loren leaned forward and peered at the photograph. "I've seen that one before." She pointed to the symbol that was my name. "It was on the dragon bone my father found."

I tilted my head to peer back at her and raised an eyebrow. "You mean the one he manufactured."

She leaned away from me with a tightened jaw

and a harsh squint. "No, he *found* it and then he *copied* it. Much like taking a photograph. Or like a famous Italian artist we both know."

I rolled my eyes and leaned my head back in my chair. The headache was returning. Loren snatched the photo out of my hands.

"But in the bone my father copied, there were other symbols around it," she said. "No one could decipher them. They'd never seen characters like them before."

I'd only heard the story of Dr. Van Alst and his fake bone. I'd never actually seen what he'd faked. "Loren, do you have a picture of the bone your father ... *found*?"

"I do." She pulled out her phone and tapped at the screen.

After a few seconds, Loren handed over her phone. I stared at the grainy picture of a turtle shell with etchings at the center. Again, I made out my name, which meant whatever Dr. Van Alst had copied this from had been the real deal. What were the odds? And why, again, hadn't he simply taken the artifact with him instead of making a copy? I asked Loren that very question.

"He said he tried." She toyed with her phone,

running her thumb across the face of the image. "But he was stopped."

"By who?"

"Locals." She met my eyes this time. There was sorrow there. Dr. Van Alst had died only a few years ago, and the pain was still fresh in his daughter's heart.

The glistening in Loren's eyes told me she wanted to talk about it, but her stiff upper lip told me I'd have to ask. I had lost more friends than I cared to count over the centuries. It was why I avoided making new ones. I decided to stop my prodding of Loren and turned my attention back to the bone.

With a new focus, I saw that the etchings on Dr. Van Alst's copy weren't exactly my name. The character for my name looked like a modern-day U with a slash at the top. But there was a line slashed at an odd angle that wasn't quite right. I couldn't tell if it was dust on the celluloid, or a mistake I may have made when I etched it, or maybe Dr. Van Alst had simply copied it wrong. Also on this bone were the same two characters that I couldn't make out on Loren's bone.

"I can't tell what these two characters are," I said,

holding up the picture of the first bone next to Loren's cell phone. "They're unknown to me."

"My father looked up every symbol known to man, but he couldn't determine them either. It looks like a mix of ancient Chinese and Aramaic, but how could that be? The Chinese had no contact with people from the Middle East at that time."

I shut my eyes and slowly inhaled as the light of truth shone before me. Loren was wrong. The ancient Chinese did have contact with people who wrote and spoke Aramaic.

When I opened my eyes again, it was all crystal clear. If I looked at the characters again with a new perspective, I could see that I did know them. Loren was observant. She just didn't know what she was looking at.

Mixed in with the ancient Chinese script were Aramaic numbers. There were the characters for the number five and number six, which were Epsilon and Vau. The two Immortal lovers who hadn't been seen for nearly two millennia.

CHAPTER TWENTY

The dream gripped me hard. But this time, I wasn't on a cold, stone table with a jade blade hanging over my chest. There were no men in black surrounding me, crowding in on me like parasites hungry for my blood. There were no bones breaking or cries of children or wails of women. No, in this dream there was laughter.

In my mind, I opened my eyes to a bright, sunny day. Greenery enveloped me as far as the eye could see. I was in a forest. Off in the horizon, I saw mountains covered in foliage. I smelled the water in the wind, as well as on the fertile ground.

The tinkling of laughter came nearer, followed by a deep-bellied laugh. I wanted to run to greet the joy in the air, but I knew I had to hold still and watch.

Soon, figures made their way out of the forest. A woman dressed in colorful robes ran out of the trees. Her long, dark hair moved like a curtain of water as she ran. She kept looking over her shoulder. Her eyes sparkled as she caught sight of the large man who gave chase. In a matter of two steps, he ate up the distance between them.

The man swept her up in his huge arms and spun her around. The woman threw her head back and laughed. She slid slowly down his body and, when she was close enough, latched her smiling lips onto his grinning ones.

My chest hurt as I watched the happy couple. I knew these two. Had known them for most of a life that I now couldn't remember. They were Epsilon and Vau.

Vau broke the kiss, smiling down with pure love and joy at Epsilon. Her light eyes looked up and caught mine. Smile spreading, her hand waved at me.

"Come, Tisa," she called.

Epsilon looked over his shoulder. When his gaze found mine, he gave me a sheepish grin. He set Vau's feet down on the ground and motioned with his head for me to follow them. They took off into the forest.

"Come, Tisa," I heard Vau call again.

But I couldn't move to follow them. My body shook with the effort of trying to pick up my feet. I felt moisture on my cheek. When I reached to my face, my fingers came away wet. Tears streamed from the corners of my eyes.

An arm came around me, followed by another. I didn't struggle. I felt safe, surrounded by a mountain of warmth. I snuggled back into a broad chest, turning to Tres.

But this wasn't the Tresor Mohandis I knew. This was someone else. This man looked down at me with an expression I'd never seen on Tres' face. It was a look I didn't know his face was capable of. It was tender. It was open. He was smiling.

He looked younger, if that made sense. His eyes were still obsidian black, but bright. His lips weren't cruel. They looked lush and kissable. His gaze dipped to my lips as though he saw the trajectory of my thoughts. He leaned in and brushed his lips against mine before he pulled away with a wince. Taking in a shaky breath, he laughed.

"I told you," he said, shaking his head. "Love makes you weak."

He released his arms from around me and took a step back. The openness in his eyes shuttered. His soft lips formed a hard line. I stood immobile, still unable to move my feet. I felt tethered to something hard and cold. My chest ached, and then I heard the screams.

"Love makes you weak," Tres repeated as he picked up his retreat. His face transformed into the hard veneer I now knew. His eyes hardened. He looked away from me.

I woke tangled in the sheets of the bed at the hotel room. The room was warm, but my body felt chilled. There was a slight sheen of sweat on my skin. My eyes were itchy and the tip of my nose was cold. My limbs were exhausted, as though I had been in a real struggle. We'd arrived in the Gongyi late last night, and I'd immediately come to the hotel and collapsed into the bed.

I wrapped my arms around myself now, but I couldn't get warm. I reached for my phone and dialed Zane's number, hoping for a connection. It went straight to voicemail. His voice spoke in that lilting French accent. When I reached the end of the message, I hung up, and then hit redial to hear his voice again. I repeated the pattern a few more times, cradling the phone against my cheek.

I'd been apart from Zane for twenty-four hours, but it still felt like I was in the throes of a month-long exposure to the allergy. But we'd only spent a few days together. Even when we did spend a few weeks or more together, I'd never felt more than fatigue and restlessness. I was usually on the mend by the time we'd been apart for a day. But my body was not mending like it should.

I shut down the phone and began to dress. The sun was high in the sky of a mild, late afternoon. Looking off into the distance, I spied a mountain range. I squinted, trying to determine if it was the same range as the one I'd seen in my dream. The same mountains where Epsilon and Vau had run off toward. The same mountains that I looked upon in horror as I heard the screams.

I wondered if I should turn back. My death was possible in this place. I knew the men in black were here, hiding out, waiting for the right time to strike me down … and do what? Kill me? Was it even possible? I didn't know.

But I couldn't turn away. The archaeologist in me wouldn't allow it. It was *my* voice that was lost this time. I needed to find out what I was trying to say on those bones, whether my mind wanted to give up the information or not. The dirt would tell my truth and

I would face it, whatever might come. I just needed another day to get over the allergy, then I would go down into the forests. At my full strength, I stood a fighting chance at whatever I would face.

I started at the knock on the door. When I opened it, I found Loren leaning on the doorjamb at the other side. She grimaced when she saw me. Her pretty, well-rested face contorted into a look of horror as she met my gaze.

"You look like shit," she said as she walked past me and into the room. "I brought soup."

She held up the covered platter. The smell of congee, a thick, hot rice porridge akin to chicken noodle soup, wafted to my nose. I realized how hungry I was as I snatched the dish from her and dug into the broth with a vengeance.

"Are you gonna be able to make this trek down onto the site?" Loren eyed me with real concern. "We can't get there by ATV. The only way through is on horseback, and it's a two-day journey."

"I'll be fine. It's just—"

"Allergies, you said." Loren studied me with those observant eyes. I knew she wasn't buying my excuse, but she had nothing else to go on. And I was telling the truth, even if I wasn't sneezing up a fit or hacking up my lungs.

"You know," I said after another gulp of soup, "there's nothing stopping you from going down without me."

I put the bowl to my mouth and slurped so she couldn't read any expression on my face. Still, she studied me quietly for a moment.

"There was really no reason for you to come in the first place," she said. "I don't buy that whole *truth must be told* mumbo jumbo."

I wiped at my mouth. "Why do you think I came, then?"

The bowl was empty. I had no cover. We stared each other down. After only a week of knowing each other, we let our guards down and took in a true assessment.

"I think you're insatiably curious and you want to know more about this lost civilization," Loren said. "And I think you might be one of those rare people who believes in justice."

Wow, she really was observant. I had totally pegged this woman all wrong. My initial view of Loren Van Alst was that she was a raider looking to make a quick buck. Then I'd recalculated my assessment that she was on the noble cause of righting her father's name. It looked like she was actually a good person. Someone I could possibly trust with a little more of the truth. Who might understand the real gravity behind the situation I found myself in.

And then she ruined it by opening her mouth. "Also, I think you have a girl crush on me."

I rolled my eyes, but Loren turned serious.

"It's nice having someone believe me instead of thinking I'm trying to run a scam or pass off a forgery because of my family's past." Loren didn't meet my eyes as the words rolled off her tongue.

I wanted to make a quip, but I felt the shift happening in our relationship from wary strangers to something like friendship.

"You're a cool chick, Nia Rivers."

"You're not so bad yourself, Loren Van Alst."

"It's nice to know someone has my back. That hasn't been true for me since my dad died." Her smile was awkward and her blue eyes brimmed with sincerity. Then she gave her body a shake, like a dog shaking off the sudsy waters of a bath. She plopped onto the bed and grabbed for the remote.

"Anyway, enough sap," she said. "I've been dying to watch really bad Chinese TV."

She clicked a button on the remote. A news show popped up. Loren made a face and kept going until a martial arts movie with ninjas flying high filled the screen. My body turned stiff. Beside me, Loren, who had been sitting cross-legged peering at the screen, leaned away from the action.

"Ninjas." She grimaced.

"Not a fan?" I asked.

"Not at all."

"Me neither."

She clicked a couple more times. "Oh, *The Usual Suspects* dubbed in Chinese! Score."

Loren patted the empty space on my bed. I came over and sat down beside her. On the screen, I saw Kevin Spacey's smirk as he spun a fantastical tale to Chazz Palminteri.

"That movie drives me crazy," I said. "What detective would believe such a farcical story?"

Palminteri continued to interrogate Spacey, the only survivor in a crime gone wrong. In the film, the detective digs for the truth in an increasingly complex murder-heist-mystery story. The brash detective never once guessed that the unassuming, weak, disabled man telling the tale was the mastermind behind the whole crime, until the last moment of the film when it was too late.

"All the detective has to do is turn around and the writing is clearly on the wall," I said. "Literally."

All the clues to the whodunit were posted on a

tack board at the cop's back. Keyser Söze, which translates to Mr. Talk Too Much, simply wove his tale from the wanted posters and announcements posted on the wall.

"You're probably one of those people who spends the movie trying to figure out who did it instead of enjoying the ride," Loren said. "The fun is in the twist. So sit back and let's just enjoy the movie while it lasts."

After an afternoon of cheesy American movies dubbed in Chinese, and then a night of thankfully dreamless sleep, I felt like myself again. The fatigue was gone from my bones. The bags under my eyes had packed up and left. But my heart was still heavy from the absence of Zane, and my spirit was still weary from the residue of the dreams of Epsilon and Vau.

I refused to remember the safety and security I'd felt from the other man in my dreams. After all, his arrival in the dream was what had turned it into a nightmare. It wasn't until his strong arms were holding me tight that I heard the screams. Whatever we'd had in the past, I'd forgotten it for a reason and I needed to remember that.

Loren and I spent the morning trudging around the main street of the city. There wasn't much to see. When we'd gotten off the train, it had been easy to debark as we were the only ones getting off. The other passengers either slept through the stop or took one look out the window and turned their gaze back to their phones and travel books.

Walking down the rundown streets, it was evident the people didn't get many tourists down here. They openly stared at the blonde woman and the darker-skinned woman who could have been one of their own, or something else entirely. Though they stared, no one approached us. They gave us a wide berth.

There were a few shops along the thoroughfare and a handful of restaurants. In the center of the town was its crowning jewel—a tomb. The tomb of the River Queen sat amid an otherwise unassuming park. Children ran about the grass. Older men and women went through the slow, meditative movements of Tai Chi. A few twenty-somethings pressed buttons on their outdated cell phones. No one paid too much attention to the tomb other than me.

The structure was modeled after the tombs of the Forbidden City with sloping roofs that resembled the brim of a cowboy's hat. Large stone animals sat before the tomb, presumably guarding the sleeping queen within—the mystical queen who had saved the city and its people from the devastating floods of the Yellow River so many centuries ago.

And now, centuries later, the tomb sat locked. There was no way in. I studied the barred door.

"Don't bother," Loren said. "There's nothing in there."

I turned to her with a brow raised. She shrugged in that way I was coming to know that meant *Don't ask me how I know the answer unless you want to be tried as an accomplice.* And so, I didn't.

But it was curious. If this place had been ruled by an actual queen, that would be noteworthy. Loren was right. China was not known for its female leadership in the past. In the present, that was starting to change. This temple and the stories of the River Queen put her at nearly two thousand years old. If their queen could've been a claim to fame, why weren't the people of Gongyi shouting about her presence?

It was a question I hoped to answer when we began our journey into the forest tomorrow. I'd just pile this question on top of the many others I had.

We turned from the temple and headed back to the hotel to change for dinner.

Mr. Xu lived very well for a city councilman in a small, sleepy province. His home was filled with relics and pictures of his ancestors in photographs and paintings at different points in history. The men in each rendering could've been the same man cut out and placed in a different time period. These were the Xia of history. And, to my woe, there was a resemblance to the ninja I'd unmasked back at the reflecting pool in Washington, D.C.

I shut my eyes and sighed. When I opened them, another painting stood out and grabbed my attention. It was of a woman floating above the waters. She was dressed in a deep, sea-colored blue. Her arms were outstretched. There were children on either side of the riverbank below her. They smiled up at her adoringly, and she gazed down at them with benevolence.

"That painting has your face," Loren said. She turned and peered at my features. "That seems to happen to you a lot."

She was right, kind of. The woman in the painting did have an uncanny resemblance to me.

But her features were lacking in detail. The cheekbones weren't quite right. The shape of the lips was off. The eyes didn't have the cat-like uptilt. I looked for the signature. When I found it, I noted that it was not one of Zane's aliases.

A chill ran up my spine even though the evening air and the interior of the house was warm. I had to blink a couple of times as my vision went a bit hazy. I felt a cough coming on.

A group of children ran through the hall, laughing and giggling. They came to a comedic stop, digging their heels into the ground and windmilling their arms to slow their motion, when they saw me. They gaped in awe, looking from me to the painting.

"Is that any way to treat an honored guest?"

Mr. Xu entered the receiving room. He walked slowly, leaning heavily on his cane. He seemed to have aged another decade since the last time I'd seen him only a week ago.

"Go on," he shooed them. "Up the stairs and into bed with the lot of you."

He bent down to receive hugs from a couple of the younger children. The older ones I recognized from the festival back in Beijing. These were his grandchildren. They snuck glances at me as they headed up the stairs.

"There is nothing better than seeing your future in a child's eyes." The hunch in Xu's back seemed more rounded. His wispy hair looked even more sparse. His cheeks appeared shrunken in. When he reached for me, his frail hand closed around mine and I got prickles, like a storm cloud moving across the horizon. I took a deep breath and held still when what I wanted to do was pull away, like snatching my hand away from hard ice.

"How are you feeling, Dr. Rivers?" he asked. "I understand you delayed your trip to the forests by a day due to illness? I do hope it's nothing serious."

"It was just allergies," I said. "I'm fine now." I smiled down at him before wrenching my head back and coughing.

A handkerchief appeared from behind me. I traced the length of the arm up until I met with Tresor Mohandis's face.

"What are you doing here?" I demanded, ignoring the proffered handkerchief.

"I was invited," he said, putting away the unclaimed cloth.

I turned to Mr. Xu, my feet shuffling back a step beyond the two of them.

But Mr. Xu smiled amiably, even if the smile

didn't reach his eyes. "Mr. Mohandis and I have come to an understanding."

"Mr. Xu agreed to put aside any objections from his seat as a councilman if I gave you and Ms. Van Alst time to explore the site," Tres said.

"Oh," I said, realization dawning. "So your generosity in giving Ms. Van Alst and me passage onto *your* lands was a business decision and not out of..."

I swallowed instead of finishing the sentence. I had no idea what word would have come out of my mouth. Just because I had dreams about this man holding me, making me feel safe and cherished, didn't mean I meant anything to him. And, to confirm, he spoke his truth.

"Everything I do is a business decision, Dr. Rivers." The hard mask was back in place. There was no trace of the tenderness I'd imagined and dreamed about.

"The Xia have always been forward-thinkers and adaptable," Mr. Xu said. "Even while we hold on to our past traditions. I want my homeland to prosper again, for the sake of my children and grandchildren. After all, we don't live forever, do we?"

I felt Tres' eyes on me. I steadily avoided his gaze.

There was an awkward moment of silence. But thank God for Loren and her single-minded mission to restore her father's name.

"You are forward-thinkers," Loren agreed. "As far as my father could tell, the Xia were the first Chinese dynasty to have a queen."

"Queen?" Mr. Xu asked.

Loren pointed to the painting of the woman above the river. "Yes, the River Queen."

Mr. Xu shook his head. "Queen is actually a mistranslation. She was not a mortal queen; she was an immortal goddess."

I looked again at the painting that very well could have been of me. The connections snapped together in my mind like magnets. The Chinese characters for goddess and queen began the same, but differed in the second character. How could I have missed that? More of the characters on the bone snapped into place. The Lin Kuie must've been making sacrifices *to* their goddess.

"So, there wasn't a ruling queen of the Xia?" The disappointment was palpable in Loren's voice. "She wasn't real?"

"All gods, goddesses, and myths start with a truth," said Mr. Xu. "But Pa Shui was very much real."

"Excuse me?" Tres said. "Did you say Pa Shui?"

Mr. Xu nodded.

Tres turned to me. Those dark eyes bored into mine, but I avoided his gaze.

"Shui means river," Loren said. "And Pa is the number nine." Now Loren turned to me, obviously remembering the Nova Fleuve alias from my flight manifest.

"Legend says that the goddess, Pa Shui, was sailing down the river, trying to recover from a broken heart. She came from the west and sailed to the east. She took the waters into herself, and the flood receded. Once the people were safe, she left to find her lover. But the next season, she returned with her heart broken. That is why the river often changes course. The pattern repeated. It would flood when she came to us with a broken heart, and it would recede when she was happy."

"This legend began about two thousand years ago?" Tres asked.

"I don't believe it was a legend," Xu said. "I believe it's real."

"But the floods continue to this day," Tres challenged.

"The legend says that the floods ceased once the goddess sacrificed herself for her people."

My head was spinning. We were back to a sacrifice *of* the goddess, which just didn't make any damn sense.

"There are prophecies that she will return and the floods will cease again," Xu said.

Tres opened his mouth, likely to ridicule the idea, but I cut him off. I needed to make some sense of this. And Xu was right about one thing—every story had a kernel of truth. You just had to dig. "Are these legends oral stories? Or are they written down somewhere?"

"Both," Xu answered. "My mother told me these stories. Unfortunately, she passed away a very long time ago. But she said the prophecy of the return of Pa Shui was foretold on dragon bones. Perhaps you and Ms. Van Alst will find the relics on your journey tomorrow."

A bell sounded for dinner. Mr. Xu led the way forward with Loren. I made to follow, but Tres's hand on my arm held me back.

"Goddess?" he sneered, stepping in front of me when I didn't turn to face him.

Immortals had long stopped claiming such titles with humanity. It only ever led to death and destruction. Human destruction, not our own.

"It was a long time ago," I hissed. "I don't

remember what happened." I found his hard gaze and glared at him. "What do you care, anyway?"

"I've lived long enough to know that you can forget the past, but you can't rewrite history if that's what you're trying to do."

I had no comeback for that, and he saw it. I had forgotten my fair share of pasts recently. My past with Tres, my past with Epsilon and Vau, and my past with the Xia people. But I wasn't trying to rewrite it. I was trying to recover it. Well, my past with Vau, Epsilon, and the Xia, not my past with him.

"Hey, guys."

We both turned to see Loren in the doorway to the dining area.

"Play nice," she said. "We're guests. You can take it behind closed doors later."

Tres and I sprang apart as though that was the grossest idea ever. I folded my arms over my chest. He clenched his jaw and his fists. His stiff body stood even taller as he stormed ahead of us.

Loren came to stand beside me and watch the show of him walking away. "There's *so* something there. Why are you holding out on me?"

"All that's between that man and me is mutual dislike."

"Yeah," she agreed. "But it came from somewhere. Otherwise, there would be indifference."

"I'm with Zane."

"You know my view on monogamy." Loren shrugged. "Life's too short to stay faithful. I swear, sometimes you talk like you're an old woman born in the last century."

CHAPTER TWENTY-TWO

I swung my leg over the Mongol horse. It wasn't a great feat. I was larger than the horse, which stood at about five feet. The breed was small, but they could carry heavy loads and their stamina was legendary. Genghis Khan had nearly taken over the Eastern world on the backs of these small but mighty beasts. I mounted mine, ready to delve into a past it appeared I'd purposely forgotten.

Loren pulled up beside me on her steed. Her eyes were trained past me. Her lips quivered, failing to hide a building snicker. I turned to see what she found so funny. Then I had to look away, lest I burst out in a full belly laugh.

Tresor Mohandis was not having an easy time

mounting his own steed. The two beasts faced off. Tres gripped the reins of the mongrel. The horse stepped to the side as the big man tried to mount, causing Tres, foot in stirrup, to hop alongside the horse to keep from falling over.

I lost it then, which caused a domino effect. Loren's trickle of laughter teetered from her lips. Tres looked up and glared at us. We were not cowed, especially not by a man who couldn't mount an animal that was no bigger than a cow.

Tres recovered his foot from the stirrup and tossed the reins down in frustration. "Why can't we take a helicopter?"

"Because there's nowhere to land it," Loren supplied helpfully. "And, before you ask, a Jeep or Land Rover can't get through these trees."

"A bulldozer could," Tres muttered as he finally mounted his horse through brute force. The animal neighed but took the brunt of its new master's weight and command.

Tres was decked out in expensive boots that looked like they'd never hit the concrete. His jeans looked like they'd been tailored by a brand-name designer. His linen shirt wouldn't last the day in this dirt. He would be a tousled, disheveled, worn-through mess by nightfall. And I found all that delightful.

I smiled pleasantly at him as he rode by. He narrowed his eyes as he passed me. I gave my horse a tug and followed at a distance.

We were a small party. Loren and I had come alone, but Tres brought two guides provided by Mr. Xu. The trek through the dense woods would take two days. I'd trekked through the world's most extreme climates with ease. But this was the first time I did it with another Immortal in my presence, and one I didn't care for at that.

My head was pounding by the end of the first night. It wasn't just from Tres's presence—though that factored in. His age and strength brought the recently cured allergy symptoms back with a vengeance. There was an annoying pinch between my shoulder blades. My pinky toe hurt in comfortable boots I'd worn for years. I bit my lip as we went through a tricky passage, and I tasted blood. I didn't know how humans lived with these annoyances day in and day out.

Those were all minor complaints. The screams of my nightmares pierced my waking hours. I jumped at every snapped branch, expecting men to fly out of trees and take their revenge. But the sky was cloudless, blue, and empty.

As the day stretched on, I could see much evidence of an ancient civilization. Stone structures poked their heads out of the ground. The landscape lay before me like a classroom with students raising their hands to be called on by the teacher. Archaeology was never this easy. Remains were rarely visible from a mountaintop or out in the desert sands. But, like the site in Honduras, this civilization wanted to be found.

I was certain that if we dug up this dirt, we'd find a large city beneath our feet. It was likely that the flood waters had reached inland and washed away all traces of life.

As the sun began to set, we came to a man-made structure that was nothing like the rest we'd seen all day. We stood looking at the triangular structure in the middle of the Chinese wilderness.

"Pyramids aren't uncommon in China," Loren said. "They were mostly burial mounds."

But this mound was set apart from the signs of civilization we'd found. It sat alone in what I assumed might be the center of the town. Burial sites were for the masses, not a solitary person. No, this looked like someone's home.

Loren was the first inside. The two guides stayed back. I couldn't tell if it was fear in their eyes, or something else. Tres stared at the edifice for another second. His eyes connected with mine with an unreadable expression, and then he went in.

I stepped up to the opening. The moment my foot touched the threshold, a wave of emotion nearly knocked me to my knees. Something dark bubbled in my gut and raced up into my lungs.

I grabbed onto the side of the structure. I had been here before. I looked up at the pyramid, but my eyes were unfocused as I expected to hear screams. But I didn't. Instead, I heard laughter. It was high-pitched and happy, followed by a deep baritone full of delight.

It came and went like the wind. As soon as the sound cleared from my head, the nausea receded. I still gripped the wall. My fingers roved over a groove. As I caught my breath, I noticed the groove felt like a pattern. I looked up at the wall of the doorway. What I saw had me closing my eyes again.

On the entrance were the markings of the people who must've built and lived in this dwelling. The clearly marked lines were not Chinese characters. They were Aramaic.

Turning away, I crossed my arms over myself as

the winds of memory continued to beat against the inside of my mind. The next sound I heard was not full of happiness and delight. It was accusatory.

"I may not read every language known to man," Tres said, "but I recognize the names of my people. When's the last time you saw Epsilon and Vau?"

I took a deep breath but did not release the hold I had on myself. "I don't remember."

He was so quiet for so long that I chanced a glance up at him. His dark eyes were granite—hard, cold, and unreadable. "Seems to be a trend with you."

I didn't take the bait. Instead, I looked off to where the guides stood with the horses. They were too far away to hear us, and they seemed unconcerned in any case.

"What's on those bones, Nia?"

"I don't have the complete story."

I wasn't looking up at his face. My eyes were fastened on his chest. His linen shirt had collected its fair amount of dirt, as I'd predicted. His shirt was open a few buttons, and I caught a glimpse of his strong chest. I couldn't turn away from the brown within the now-dingy white. I crossed my arms even tighter about myself to keep from going to him and laying my head against his pecs, which I knew would be pillow soft.

Instead, I looked into his gaze and told him the truth. "There was a sacrifice. I don't understand if it was *to* the River Goddess or *of* the River Goddess. It doesn't all make sense."

"Clearly you weren't sacrificed," he said. He looked back to Epsilon and Vau's home. "But maybe they were."

So he thought I might be the Xia's River Queen, too. And now he'd given voice to my latest fear ... that I may not have been the only Immortal to have been bound to that altar of my nightmares.

The wind blew. It lifted my hair, which was loose. As it blew about my face, a memory flashed before my eyes. I heard that same high-pitched, happy laughter. In my memory, I looked out at the blue sky and equally blue sea. There were sails above my head and a wheel in my hands. Beside me, Vau gave a joyful laugh as we crashed into an oncoming wave.

How had I forgotten that? It was Vau who had taught me to sail. Her tanned face and dark hair whipped about as mine did now. I held on to the vision of her in my mind. How could I have forgotten her face? We could've been sisters as we favored each other so.

I blinked myself back to the present and my knees wobbled. But I didn't hit the ground. Instead, I found myself inside of a steel cage full of warmth.

My nose turned into a chest that was soft and familiar, like my favorite pillow. As the cage closed around me I felt safe, protected, cherished. I tilted my head to look up into Tres's face. I knew this face. Like the back of my hand, like my signature, this face was familiar to me. How had I forgotten its lines and planes?

His lips were parted. His eyes widened. He was unguarded in this moment. His hand rose, and he brushed the wayward strands of hair off my temple. He'd done this before, countless times. I knew he had, but I couldn't remember a single one, only the feeling of it.

"It shouldn't hurt after all this time," he said, his voice no louder than the wind. "But when you look at me like you don't know me..."

He swallowed. I felt the lump that stuck in his throat somewhere deep in the recesses of my heart. Tres set me on my feet and turned away. His shoulders looked like boulders of tension. He stood in profile, his body angled away from me, but I saw his face. I watched his jaw tense as he turned his head up to the receding sun.

"It was because of you," I said. "I came here on a boat like Xu said. I was running from you, wasn't I?"

He said nothing. The tension mounted in his shoulder blades. His fingers clenched and unclenched.

"You broke my heart," I accused.

That got his attention. His eyes snapped open, and he whirled around to face me. His steps were thunderous as they closed the space between us. I took an involuntary step back.

"*I* broke *your* heart?" He stared at me. His mouth worked, but nothing came out. He was at a loss for words. The pain etched on his face was too much for me to look upon.

"Did you do this?" I asked. "Did you murder these people? The Xia?"

"Murder?" His face contorted in a mix of anger, disbelief, and confusion.

"I have these dreams of people being slaughtered, but not by my own hand. Was it you?"

"Wrong Immortal," he said, shaking his head slowly. All trace of tenderness from before was gone. "Murder to get what I want isn't exactly my style."

I took another step back as though his words were a missile being hurled at me and their impact would devastate.

"Your mind can reject it," Tres continued. "But like you always say, the dirt never lies."

I turned from him as his words continued to weaken the protective walls in my head, walls that were clearly erected around memories I wanted to forget. Needed to forget.

"Your memory has always been selective," Tres said. "You left him before because his temper got the better of him. I wouldn't be surprised if that's what happened here. He was always a jealous god."

I shut my eyes tight, but with each word from Tres, my defenses continued to crumble.

"And now he hides behind the veneer of a peaceful artist. He's fooled you again."

I shook my head violently, but the more I shook, the more the memories came loose. Zane's beautiful, smiling face popped into my mind as a match to Tres's words. I pushed at the vision, trying to shove it away from me. Tres was lying, or he was stretching the truth. Immortals did it all the time.

"I have never been anything but honest and upfront with you," he continued.

I whirled around then, if only to get away from the destruction within me. "Then tell me who you are to me."

Tres opened his mouth. Then he closed it. There

was an entire world swirling within the depths of his eyes, one I'd been to before but couldn't seem to get back to.

"Like I said," he said, "some things are better left buried beneath the dirt." And, with that, he turned and stormed off to his horse.

CHAPTER TWENTY-THREE

"You okay?" Loren asked the next morning as we broke camp.

"Yeah," I said. But I'm sure I looked like the pile of horse dung whose smell was wafting over to our campsite. "It's just—"

"Allergies," Loren cut me off as she stuffed her sleeping bag into its liner. Her tone spoke volumes—she wasn't buying the excuse any longer. She probably never had. "That keeps happening to you, but only when you've been around Fine Frenchy and Broody Billionaire. I'm starting to wonder if you're allergic to men you find attractive, which would be the weirdest form of birth control I've ever heard of."

Loren was in the wrong career. She should give up tomb raiding. Clearly, her talent was elsewhere.

The girl should be a contestant on a game show where people solved puzzles for money.

"We're just half a day's ride to where I found the bones," she said. "Then this will all be over. I'll prove my father was telling the truth, and you'll get to rescue another lost culture from the bowels of the earth."

I dragged myself to my mount. My limbs felt heavy. One of the guides Mr. Xu provided handed me the reins of my horse. His fingertips accidentally brushed mine as the leather straps exchanged hands. My fingers cramped around the lead. I clenched and unclenched them a couple of times before mounting the horse. The guide smirked at my hands before turning and mounting his own steed.

I glared over at Tres, who I knew was the source of my discomfort. The pinch had returned to that place between my shoulder blades. The headache was a gong against my cranium. It was his age as an Immortal, and his general demeanor as an asshole of biblical proportions, that had me in this bad way.

But glancing over at him, I saw he was rubbing at a spot behind his neck, too. His face contorted in discomfort. His eyes were a bit red from what I assumed was lack of sleep. Was I having the same effect on him?

It didn't make sense. I could stay with Zane for days before the weariness set in. It was always weeks before I began to lose my strength. Why was Tres having this effect on me? And why was I apparently having the same effect on him after only two days?

During the half day it took to reach the site, I felt every clomp of the horse over the rough terrain. A quick glance over at Tres showed that he pinched at his shoulder blades every now and then, but clearly the allergy wasn't bothering him as much as it was taking a toll on me. He hadn't been around three of his own kind in the span of a week, nor plagued by nightmares of his past, trying desperately to hold waking memories at bay.

As the sun rose to its peak, we arrived. The site we pulled into was on a hillside. We were nearer to the river waters. I smelled the dampness in the air and the dirt as we dismounted. A chill ran through me in the windless day. I'd been here before.

The guides stayed back, insisting they needed to keep an eye on the horses while we went in. I kept hearing the fish-headed alien from that space movie saying, "It's a trap." But I had to go forward. I couldn't hold back the truth any longer, whatever it may be.

I looked around at the entrance to the caves.

They didn't look familiar, but I knew I'd been here before. My feet rooted to the earth, and something inside me told me to turn back. Something dark pushed at the lock in my mind, urging its way free.

I wrapped my arms around myself like I'd done outside of Epsilon and Vau's home. I didn't want to go into that cave any more than I'd wanted to go into the pyramid. I knew that once I crossed the threshold, there was no turning back. Whatever I'd locked away inside myself was going to come back to the forefront.

"They're in there," Loren said, nudging me forward.

I took a deep breath and took the first step, then another, and then another. Tres and Loren marched steadily forward ahead of me. Loren disappeared into the darkness of the entrance, and my heartbeat increased. I hesitated at the threshold.

Tres tossed a look over his shoulder at me, raising an eyebrow. There was accusation, curiosity, and concern in his gaze. I couldn't deal with any of his emotions. So instead of facing him, I made my way inside.

The darkness assaulted me immediately. I nearly turned back into the receding daylight. Tres held up a high-beam lantern. My eyes adjusted quickly as I looked around.

The humidity in the cave was high, the temperature a cool sixty degrees. Prime conditions to preserve ancient artifacts for hundreds of years. There were writings all over the walls. I could tell that these were names and not a story. They also were not by my hand.

It looked as though many people had taken a hand at writing them. It reminded me of the Vietnam Wall Memorial in Washington, D.C. I expected this was the same type of memorial. Probably a record of the names of those who had been born, or those who had fallen. There were hundreds, male and female, etched into the walls.

"They're down here," Loren said.

She led us down a narrow passageway. The further we went, the more light came in. I looked up and could see that there was an opening in the cave that brought in natural light like a skylight.

Glancing back at the narrow passage, I noted there was only one way in and one way out. If anyone came up behind, we were trapped. I cursed under my breath, but I kept going. My feet wouldn't stop moving, just as my brain wouldn't stop turning.

I'd been here before … and not just in my nightmares. In reality.

"Here." Loren pointed ahead. "There they are."

I made out turtle shells, ox scapula, and various other mammalian bones. I had expected the bones to be buried. Or mounted on the walls. They weren't. They sat on a bit of raised earth, much like a set of trophies mounted on a mantel. And like trophies, these could be easily lifted and carried from their viewing place.

I turned back to Loren. "I thought you said you couldn't take the bones with you."

"Trust me, I couldn't."

I narrowed my eyes at her. "You said you couldn't get the bones out. You said your father couldn't get the bones out either. Why not? What stopped you? Or rather … who stopped you?"

She shook her head. "You wouldn't believe me if I told you."

I took a deep breath before I said the word I'd kept to myself for hundreds of years. "Ninjas?"

Loren blinked those blue eyes wide. "Or maybe you *would* believe me."

My gaze shifted from Loren's and went to the solitary way in and out. It was still empty, but I knew that wouldn't last long. The Lin Kuie had to be near.

They were probably waiting on the outside of the cave.

"Flying ninjas," Loren said. "I mean, these dudes were straight out of *House of Flying Daggers* high-wire martial arts, but the thing is, there were no wires."

Tres came up between us. Unlike the hushed awe of Loren's voice, his was his normal deep-set, impatient, annoyed tone. "What do the bones say?"

Loren narrowed her eyes at his interruption. I turned back to the bones. There were three of them. The one Loren had taken the picture of and shown me in Washington, D.C. On its right was one I hadn't seen before. On the far side of those two was—

"That's the one my father found," Loren said. She crouched down and reached for it but withdrew her fingers at the final second. "Do you see? It's real. He was telling the truth. But the ninjas wouldn't let him take it. Who was going to believe that? Ninjas in a cave. So he copied it. After he died, I found this place. I came here, and they pulled the same thing with me. They wouldn't let me take it, but they let me go. Luckily, the times had changed and I had a camera phone. But I only had a chance to take a picture of the one bone."

I stared at the raised platform that the bones

were mounted on. It didn't look like a natural structure. It looked man-made. I looked around at the inside of the cave. It was well-kept, as though someone had been in here recently and frequently. And then I saw it.

Off in the recesses of the cave, it was there. Just like I'd seen in my nightmares. It looked smaller in the light from the sky. But the chills that ran down my back were just as strong as the ones that woke me in the middle of the night. In the corner sat the altar of my nightmares.

I reached for the cool, comfortable steel of the dagger at my hip as I looked back at the entryway. It was empty, but I still felt the prickles.

"Nia," Tres said. "What do the bones say?"

Something wasn't right here. But I'd suspected that all along, hadn't I? I just had to figure out what.

Had I mentioned I hated riddles?

I turned my back from the only escape route and picked up the first bone. My hands trembled under its light weight. In my mind, I saw water dropping on the bone. I knew they were my tears. I'd cried as I wrote on these carcasses. But the water had long ago evaporated and only the symbols remained. The first bone that Loren's father had found told the beginning of the story. The bone Loren had presented to me was the end with my signature. And now I had the last bone, which was the middle of the story, the worst part. What I read chilled me to my bones.

I closed my eyes. My fingers traced the symbol for the name of my friend. That joyous trickle of laughter sailed through my ears on a clear memory.

Vau.

"It's not me." I opened my eyes, but I didn't focus on either of my companions. I didn't focus on anything except the truth of what the bones told me —a truth I had written down and then buried in my mind. "I wasn't the River Goddess."

CHAPTER TWENTY-FOUR

"Uh, you thought you were the River Queen?" Loren asked the question like a mother inquiring after her child's imaginary friend.

I glanced at her, unsure where to begin to explain. There were Immortals who kept humans as servants. They informed these humans of everything, about who and what we were. Some Immortals had entire bloodlines of servants who stayed with them for generations. I'd never taken to the practice. But Loren was in this deep, and with no other way out of this cave, it seemed only fair that I bring her into the fold.

I turned my back to her and slid the collar of my shirt down over my shoulder. "Do you see that symbol?"

She leaned in and peered at the branded number on my shoulder. "That's the same as the one on the bone."

I readjusted my top and turned back around. "It's my signature. It's how I've signed every document or scroll since I learned to write. The reason I knew the dragon bone was authentic back in Washington is because I recognized my signature"—I took a deep breath and prepared for the kicker—"from two thousand years ago."

Loren blinked, and then her eyes got wide. She opened her mouth, but when no words came out, she closed her lips and her mouth went slack. She rubbed at her eyelids. Then she rubbed at her slackened jaw. She didn't argue or try to make excuses. She took the news like a grown woman.

"I'm immortal," I continued. "I'm super strong. I can't be hurt or get sick. Unless I'm near another of my kind for too long."

Her gaze flicked to Tres. She jerked her thumb. "Him, too?"

I nodded. "Yes, he's one of us as well."

"And Frenchy, too?" She huffed and rolled her eyes. "Allergies, my ass."

The girl was perceptive, I'll give her that.

"Flying ninjas and immortals," she said. "What next? Dragons? Werewolves?"

"Nia," came Tres's impatient voice. "What do the bones say?"

I fixed my gaze on Tres. "It was Vau. She's the one who came to China with a broken heart."

"During one of the times she and Epsilon broke up," Tres supplied.

I nodded. I had heard her laughter in my head, but now I was seeing flashes of her tears. We'd gone sailing during one of her breakups with Epsilon. I remembered her dark hair, so like mine, flowing behind her as she took command of the wheel. I lay on the deck beside her. Our sun-toasted skin dried under the day's light, and we talked about giving up on love. We stopped in Persia and I goaded her to come with me, but she wanted to continue north. I'd told her I'd make my way north through the Persian Royal Road, a trade route that would later become the Silk Road.

I had met up with Vau years later. She and Epsilon had made up. He'd found her. They were living in bliss in their pyramid home, surrounded by a small tribe of humans who knew what they were and what they could do. For generations, these humans had worshiped them both like gods. I remembered leaving them, promising to return soon.

"Vau came here," I said. "She saved the Xia from the flood, and they claimed her as their savior and goddess."

Tres shook his head, not needing me to complete the rest of the story. "Let me guess ... Epsilon eventually joined her. They lived here together until they grew weak."

That was what Tres had said to me in my dreams. *Love makes you weak.*

His jaw worked as he stared at me. His expression was unreadable.

I nodded. "They lived here for hundreds of years, and they grew weak. And when they could no longer protect the Xia from the floods, the people turned on them and—"

"And sacrificed them," Tres finished. His voice was small and hollow. It sounded wrong on such a mountain of a man.

He came and laid a hand on my shoulder. Instead of it making me feel weak, it felt as though he passed on some of his strength. I doubt either of us knew how to process what we were feeling. We'd seen countless numbers of humans die. But there had never been an Immortal death.

"I came back, but it was too late." I ran my finger over my signature.

I'd taken the time to write out this story and its warning, but why hadn't I taken these records with me? Why had I left them here in this cave? And why were they on display instead of buried in the dirt?

"What does it say?" Tres asked.

The answer was pushing its way to the forefront of my brain, but I refused to acknowledge it. It was simply too gruesome. Instead, my mind was taken back to my nightmares. But I didn't have to go too far. I was standing in the reality of those dark dreams. Everything was out in the open in this cave, with the light of day shining on them—the bones, the writing on the wall, the altar in the corner.

The altar.

In my mind, I saw myself on the altar. My hands and wrists were tethered. I was weak, so weak, even though there were no Immortals around. There were just dozens and dozens of humans—ninjas in black.

I'd been strapped down to that altar. I remembered the cold grip on my ankles and wrists. I'd nearly died just as Epsilon and Vau had. But I hadn't. Everyone else died. Screams tore through throats, then heads rolled. There was blood, so much blood.

I jumped as a hand settled on my shoulder. Loren held up her hands as I turned to her with my dagger raised. "Hey, I'm a friend, not a foe. Remember?" She lowered her hands. "You looked like you were about to pass out."

I lowered the dagger. My hand trembled, too weak to maintain the grip. The dagger fell to the ground.

"Nia?" Loren's face was full of concern.

"I did this. I'm the reason all those names are on that wall. I'm the reason they're all dead."

"Those savages murdered two of our kind," Tres said. "If you did anything to avenge them, it was rightful."

"Two wrongs don't make a right," I said.

Tres shook his head. "Good and bad are such human notions."

I frowned as he repeated Aleph's words back to me. My gaze caught Loren's. Her hand remained lightly at my back. I felt that without her support, I would topple over.

"I'm not convinced these people died by your

hand." Tres looked at the writing on the wall of the named dead. "This has Set written all over it."

Set was the name of the war god of Egypt. It was also a name for the number seven, which was Sept in French, Zayin in Hebrew. But Zane was a pacifist. In the entire five hundred years I'd known him, he'd never so much as raised his hand to harm another living soul. He was too preoccupied with beauty to cause any destruction.

"Zane would never—" I began.

But the words stuck in my throat as the memories gave one final push and the floodgate opened. I saw Zane's face contorted into something ugly. His beautiful eyes shining with rage. His lush lips covered in blood.

"No." The word bubbled up out of my heart, but the memories strangled the sound.

"Still defending him." Tres snorted. "Just like in Giza."

Giza? I remembered Zane holding me in the bed back in Beijing. He'd been musing over when we'd met in the sands of Giza. He'd laughed at his lapse in memory. But it hadn't been his lapse. It had been mine.

I'd forgotten him. Just like I'd forgotten Tres. My world felt like it was crumbling around me.

"Leave it," Tres said. "Whatever story it tells, leave it buried. No one needs to know any of this."

Loren and I turned and looked at him.

"There's Aramaic in those writings." He pointed to the bones. "There's no proof that anyone from the Middle East or Africa came to Asia that long ago. What will you tell the humans? That you're an Immortal and you wrote on these bones nearly two thousand years ago? Who'll believe you? Let's just destroy it all and be done with it."

"You mean silence them again," I said. "The people, and Vau and Epsilon?"

Loren took a step forward toward the bone that cost her family everything. Tres barely spared her a glance. To him, she was an insignificant speck that would be gone in less than a hundred years. That time was a weekend vacation to someone as old as him.

"Who does it help to reveal this information?" he asked. "Who does it hurt to keep it silent?"

"You," I said. "It helps you if we keep this silent. Because you want to build on this land."

He stared. "Is that really what you think?"

"For all intents and purposes, I've just ground truthed this site. I've validated the findings here. I've dated the artifacts. It's of historical record. When the antiquities society learns about this place, it's going to put a wrench in your plans of progress."

"You are the wrench in my plans, Theta," he shouted, his anger echoing off the walls of the cave. "It's always you."

I stood still until the echoes died down. "So this is about us?"

"There is no us." Tres turned as though to leave, but then stopped and turned back. "Do you think you're the only one of us who has ever done something they regret? You chose to forget. Our memories are a choice. Especially for you, who chooses to write everything down. Did you write about us?" He didn't wait for a response. He shook his head in answer and continued. "No, you didn't. Because you wanted to forget. You can't dig up someone's history in the present and drag everyone through the past."

Tres glared at me, but those obsidian eyes were transparent. The pain on his face tore at my heart. It loosened more memories of him. Hazy images of him looking down at me with the glow of adoration on his face. But then he shuttered himself, and the window into my past closed.

"Whatever," he said. "Take what you want, but I'm bulldozing this place in a couple of days."

"Not so fast, Mr. Mohandis."

The entryway I'd stopped paying attention to was now filled with the hunched frame of Mr. Xu.

"Well done, Ms. Van Alst," said Mr. Xu. "You've brought her exactly where I wanted her."

CHAPTER TWENTY-FIVE

My head whipped around to my new friend. "What the hell, Loren?"

Loren removed her hand from my back, and I wobbled. She held up both her hands, but not in a stop motion. This time, it was in a move that looked like a bid for patience.

"I told you," she said. "He recommended I bring you here to ground truth the site and decipher the bones. I don't know why he's here now or how he was able to get down through the forest at his age."

Xu straightened himself from his hunch. He cracked his neck left and then right, and stood at his full height. It was as though fifty years shed off his person. His hazy eyes twinkled and his perpetually cheerful grin transformed into something dark.

"Oh, great," Loren muttered. "More super humans. Exactly what my day needed. If he starts howling at the moon or breathing fire, I swear I'm outta here."

"You are so like your father," Xu said to Loren. "He snuck into these caves trying to exploit my heritage as well. And my sons sent him out empty-handed."

"Your sons?" Loren asked. "The ninjas?"

Xu nodded. "It's a shame what happened to your father's reputation."

Loren's fingers gripped the strap of her saddle bag. It wasn't the Vintage Gucci she normally carried. This one was nondescript and well-worn. It looked old and well-used. It also looked like it belonged to a man and not a woman. It had probably belonged to her father.

I had an idea of what might be inside the bag's depths. Reaching over to put a hand to Loren's wrist as she went for the bag's latch, I gave her a meaningful look. She gritted her teeth, but she heeded my warning.

"We've had a few visitors to these caves but never the one we wanted to return. Until now." Xu's gaze turned to me.

He approached me without his cane. I had to

stop myself from taking a step back. The prickling sensation I'd felt every time I was around him increased like bees buzzing in my ears. On the walls of the cave, under the waning light of the sun peeking in through the opening, I saw shadows moving. We were being surrounded by men dressed in black with sashes tied around their waists. Dozens of blades glinted in the fading sun rays.

I felt Tres close in on my right side. Loren flanked my left. I faced Xu.

"Pa Shui, you are home at last." Xu executed a perfect bow to me. "Do you know who I am?"

I stared into his eyes, searching for recognition. "I have to assume you are who you said you are, which is the descendant of the Xia people." I waved my hand vaguely at the wall of names behind him.

Mr. Xu shook his head. "I'm not a descendant of those people. I am those people."

I stared at him, trying to figure out what his words meant. My brain knew the answer, but once again, I shut my eyes to the truth. The reality was far worse than any nightmare.

Xu turned his attention to Tres with less reverence. "And the consort who perpetually breaks your heart, causing you so much pain."

Tres huffed and rolled his head skyward. "You got the wrong one."

I actually wasn't so sure that Tres had broken my heart. I couldn't remember him, but I was remembering what had happened here two thousand years ago.

I remembered sitting and watching it all play out before me as I lay bound to the altar. I'd come back to find Vau and Epsilon's home empty and deserted. There was no information about where they might have gone. Vau always left me a sign so that I could find her.

It had been nearly one hundred years since my last visit. That would mean at least two generations of humans had been born, and more transitioned. I had doubted if this new generation still worshiped the dark-haired goddess who came from the river.

I was wrong. They remembered Vau. They took one look at me and thought I was the goddess returning from death. It didn't strike me at first that they'd think Vau had died. Humans couldn't understand our immortality.

"When you came to our shores two thousand years ago, it brought forth a time of great prosperity for the Xia," Xu said. "Your death signaled the end of those times."

"It wasn't a death," I said. "It was murder."

"You were reborn," Xu insisted. "As a goddess, you can never truly die. The waters rebirthed you, and now you've come back to us once more."

That was what the middle bone had told, that these people believed that their River Goddess would be reborn after her sacrifice. But Vau hadn't sacrificed herself to the waters for the people. She had sacrificed her immortality for love.

I remembered it all now. I'd returned to China with a broken heart of my own to find that Vau and Epsilon had grown weak from staying together and loving each other. They'd lost their immortality and their strength. They'd become human.

The next year, when the floods came, neither Vau nor Epsilon had the strength to keep the people safe. Many lives were lost to the flood. The following season, the people turned on their gods. That was the story I'd written on the bones. I had come back to find that the people had sacrificed Vau and Epsilon.

Love makes you weak.

Epsilon and Vau had loved each other. They'd sacrificed their power to be together, and they'd paid the ultimate price. And when the new generation of Xia saw me, they thought I was her. They thought they were saved. They'd overpowered me and strapped me down to that altar.

My eye flicked to the altar. It was all coming to pass. For hundreds of years, I'd been afraid of this very scenario, of being trapped in this cave and surrounded. I'd sweated it out in my sleep and woken up to guilt and shame. I'd believed I had deserved those wretched emotions because I had done something wrong.

Now, looking at the maniacal glint in Xu's eyes, I saw the truth. The true history had been twisted and distorted until it looked nothing like the facts. But it still didn't explain how Xu and these ninjas had gained their strength and long lives.

Then I remembered what the Lin Kuie would say to me. I remembered the apothecary back in Beijing offering me that teacup steeped in dragon bones. *Your bones for our blood.*

"It was the bones," I said. "You drank Vau and Epsilon's bones."

"The Xia began the practice of drinking dragon bones," Xu confirmed. "My ancestors drank your bones out of respect. They did not expect you to gift us with your powers."

"What?" Loren gagged. "Ew, ew."

So Xu and his family had a touch of immortality

in them. It was why they'd been able to go toe to toe with me. It was why I felt weak when I faced any of them, including the children.

"But the power wanes generation to generation," he continued. "We were overjoyed when you came back to us two thousand years ago to bless us once again with your bones ... until your consort came looking for you."

Again, Xu's ire turned to Tres.

"I was a child when you came through and massacred my entire race. I remember the glint of your blade slicing through my father's neck. The blood that ran like water. I remember watching helplessly as my mother held me tight to her chest and ran for our lives."

Tres shook his head. "Wasn't me."

It hadn't been Tres. I remembered the angry roar of the warrior who wielded that blade. I remembered his eyes. I remembered his long fingers as they slashed torsos and necks as expertly as he drew a line with a pencil or chipped away at marble. I saw his lip, that usually curled in a devious smile, contorted in a sneer of outrage.

Xu had it all so twisted. I didn't know how to start unraveling it all. He'd confused me with Vau. He was confusing Zane and Tres. The two favored each other a bit, but if Xu had been a child over a thousand years ago, it would be easy for him to forget the details. I'd lived longer than that and I'd forgotten Tres entirely. Zane, too, it would seem.

"Your bones will rejuvenate me," Xu said, "and fuel the blood of my children long into the future. We will be the gods who walk the earth. The Xia will reclaim our dynasty and take our rightful place in the world."

"Your bones for our blood," the Lin Kuie all said in unison. And then they moved in. There were at least fifty of them, likely more.

I felt Tres at one side and Loren at the other. There was a sea of men dressed in black. Their faces were uncovered. They all had the same face, like they were clones.

"These are my sons," Xu said. "You've met many of them in the past. They tried to bring you here peacefully."

"By attacking me under the cover of night so that you could sacrifice me and drink my bones?"

"Sacrifice? No, this is worship. This is an expression of reverence to our goddess."

No. No, it wasn't. I knew what it was like to be worshiped. But then, I had to scratch that. The man who had purported to worship me had committed genocide in my name. I didn't want that brand of admiration either.

But I'd have to deal with Zane later. First, there was the horde of ninjas advancing toward me. They claimed worship, but they were as good as tomb raiders, only the tomb they were trying to raid was my entire being. Not happening.

I rolled my neck. The twinge between my shoulder blades increased as the ninjas moved in. Their tainted blood pressed in on me. I heard Vau's laughter in my ears. I saw her eyes light as she turned the wheel of a ship. And then her voice was silenced in the wind of the sea.

"Loren, stay behind us," I said.

"Yeah, right." Loren snorted, flipping the latch of her father's pack. "I'm no one's damsel. And they'll make me as dead as they plan to make you."

She had a point.

She reached into her pack and pulled out her cane. With a hard shake, it extended. With the push of a button, a blade speared through the tip. Yeah, Loren was no damsel in this moment of distress.

The three of us stood in a loose triangle.

Tres took a step back. His heel planted beside mine as he sank himself into a horse-riding stance. I found that comical when he'd had so much trouble with his mount for the past two days. Coming toward him were the two guides Xu had provided for our trek.

Tres didn't wait for them to approach him. He took two steps, and that was all the distance his long legs needed to cover to strike first one guide, then the other, in the jaw with his booted heel. The two men's heads spun 180 degrees in opposite directions. Blood and teeth spurted across the floor as their bodies collapsed. They were no match for the strength of an Immortal his age.

The problem was they were only two out of dozens. The ninjas advanced from all sides.

I reached down for the sais at my hip just in time for the first attacker. He flew at me—literally leaped into the air and flew at me. I ground my heel into the dirt as his blade clanked against mine. With my energy drained, he actually was able to nudge my stance a foot backward.

He retracted his blade and sliced at me again. I leaped back and narrowly missed the tip of his sword. Behind me, I heard a clatter. Out of the corner of my eye, I caught two more ninjas advancing with their blades raised.

I ducked the first attacker's blade, dropped my sais, and reached into my boots. Coming up with daggers in both palms, I threw them at the two advancing fighters. The daggers hit their mark.

But a second later, the wind changed and I felt the boot of the first ninja in my back. I had to roll to evade his sword. Unfortunately, my sais was behind him. His blade glinted as he rose it above my heart.

My life didn't flash before my eyes. That would've taken too long. Instead, I heard Vau's laughter. I saw her smile. I remembered all the times we stood by each other when times got hard and our hearts grew heavy. A terrible ache opened in me as the memories of the friend I'd lost and forgotten returned to my mind.

The ninja on top of me doubled over with an "Oof." The whooshing of a cane slicing the air sounded from above, followed by a loud crack as Loren struck the man down. She kicked my sais to me, gave me a wink and a grin, and then turned to head back into the fray.

I grasped the end of my sais and stood on wobbly feet. Three more ninjas made their way to me. As I prepared to face them, everything slowed down as I looked out at the scene before me.

Tres kicked and punched out at a group of five ninjas. Heads rolled, blood splattered, screams ricocheted across the cave's walls. They fell one by one like toy soldiers. But another regiment swiftly moved in to take their places.

This time, there were ten. And another ten stood at the ready behind them. There was no way Tres could take down that many skilled fighters with Immortal powers.

Loren struck one ninja in front of her, but a second man caught her at her waist from behind and raised his dagger, aiming for her neck. Mr. Xu waited patiently by the altar, his eyes on me. And still the three men made their way toward me.

There was no way out. I couldn't wake myself from this nightmare. I was trapped in the truth of this reality. And the worst part, aside from the imminent death of my new friend and the sacrificing of the lover I was just starting to remember, was that no one would know. My voice was about to be silenced, and there would be no one to tell my story.

CHAPTER TWENTY-SIX

They locked my hands and feet with steel and then tied me to Tres, who was similarly bound in steel. It was a smart move, as we had an aversion to each other. But even though I felt weak from the abundance of Immortal half-breeds surrounding us, there was a comfort in Tres's warm heat at my back.

There were still a good twenty or so ninjas who had survived the battle. They went about the cave preparing for the sacrifice. They built a fire in one corner. Another group brought in water from the outside. It looked like they were going to get their drink on right after the sacrifice.

Tres sighed, leaning his head back. "This is why we keep the secret of our existence. Humans can't handle the fact there is anything higher than them on the food chain."

"So you're like some kind of goddess?" Loren lay in front of me. Her arms and feet were tied with ropes. Her bound hands rested on her belly. She looked up at the crack in the top of the cave where the sunlight spilled in. The sun was moving lower on the horizon. It would be nightfall soon.

"Immortal," I answered. Despite what Tres said, I figured Loren might as well know the whole truth now that we were about to die. "We're not gods, but we're not exactly human either. We don't know what we are."

"So, Broody Billionaire over here broke your heart?" Loren jerked her head to Tres.

"Broody Billionaire?" protested Tres.

"Then, when you were reborn, he came to find you here a couple thousand years ago, saw them trying to sacrifice you, and went crazy on these people?"

I felt Tres huff behind me. "I did not—" But then he slumped and gave up.

"We don't reincarnate," I said.

I paused, realizing I had no idea what happened when we died. I wondered if Vau and Epsilon had been reborn and were now somewhere on the planet trying to find each other. Maybe Vau was even trying to find me.

"It wasn't me they killed," I continued. "Xu's got it wrong. His parents' people sacrificed two other Immortals, and he thinks it's the two of us. It's all twisted up in his old mind. I can't really blame him. It's hard enough trying to keep things straight as an Immortal. Mix us in with humans, and it would appear you get a psychopath." I leaned back into Tres. "I'm sorry you got involved in this."

I didn't think he was going to respond, but after a moment, I felt him shrug. "You've blamed me for plenty of stuff in the past—stuff I actually did do. Being blamed for something I didn't do? This is new."

"She blamed you for something you didn't do?" Loren asked with false incredulity. "Glad it's not just me. Did you think I Keyser Söze-d you? You're the one who didn't tell me there were real ninjas after you."

"She didn't tell me either," Tres said.

"Well, you didn't tell me that it was ninjas who chased you out of here," I aimed at Loren. "And I haven't seen you in hundreds of years," I threw over my shoulder to Tres.

"So which one of you has a plan of escape?"

Loren said as she jackknifed her wrists in their bindings. There wasn't any give in the rope.

Neither Tres or I said anything as we watched her struggle.

"Hellooo?" Loren said after a moment of silence. She stared at both of us in turn, her eyebrows raising as neither of us offered up a plan. "We're not going out like this, are we?"

I couldn't see a way out. We were bound and surrounded. Even if there was a way to call for help, we were out in the middle of nowhere.

"They have nothing to say, Ms. Van Alst, because they see that their time is up for this lifetime. But don't worry about them; they'll be reborn. You, on the other hand ... On the bright side, you'll get to see your father again."

Loren's fingers clenched into fists in her bindings. She gritted her jaw. Her eyes fell to her father's bag, which lay discarded across the room.

Mr. Xu came to me. He was no longer hunched or limping now that he'd shed the act of his ancient age. The archaeologist in me bubbled with a ton of questions for him. When did he start physically aging? Did he get weak being around his children? How had he kept his immortality, and his family's long lives, a secret all these centuries?

But there was no time for questions. Xu reached down and unbound me from Tres while two of his ninja offspring held blades to Tres's throat. I saw Tres's hand stress the steel bindings, but they did not give. His gaze locked on mine. His dark irises were harder than the steel holding him captive.

I knew without him speaking that he wanted me to lash out at Xu. To ignore the blades whose tips drew out twin trickles of blood at either side of his neck. But then they would kill him, and Loren, and then proceed to sacrifice me anyway. There had to be another way.

"Listen to me," I said to Xu. "There are more of us out there—more Immortals. If you do this, they'll find out and come after you."

"No one, besides the two of you, has come after me in the last two millennia."

Damn, good point. We'd gotten so good at hiding ourselves. "That's because they didn't know. I didn't tell."

But I had told this time. Zane knew where I was. He would come. He'd be too late, but he'd come looking when I didn't show up in France.

"By the time anyone comes looking for you," Xu said, "I'll have amassed an army of immortal children. The Lin Kuie will come out of the forests.

We will no longer be ghosts; we will be kings. Finally, our history, our true history, will be told. Everyone will worship you and await your next birth."

"You're crazy." I shook my head, giving up any more attempts to reason with him.

No sooner were the words out of my mouth than my head jerked to the side and I felt blinding pain in my cheek. Xu had cracked me across my face with the blunt end of a sword. It was disorienting. I felt warm liquid crawl down my cheek. It wasn't tears; it was blood.

So much for reverence. Xu shoved me onto the altar. I was still too dazed to do much more than open my eyes. And when I did, I wanted to close them again. I was in the nightmare that had plagued me for nearly two thousand years.

My bound hands were pulled over my head. My bound legs were pulled downward onto the altar. This time, there were only two screams—Tres's and Loren's.

I couldn't see the blood on my face, but I felt its thick heat. Xu walked up with the business end of the blade raised above his head. I looked up and saw it was the same jade blade from my nightmare come into my reality.

I thought of the mole tied to Aleph's gardening table. Would I squeal like it had? Would the light go out of my eyes? Would my flesh be discarded in the weeds and taken back into the earth?

The men began to chant, "Your bones for our blood."

It rang in my ears, drowning out Tres's growls and Loren's screams. The blade glistened under the rising moonlight. It was the last light I'd ever see. I shut my eyes to it as the chant rang louder in my ears.

And then, in the midst of the chant, there was an "Oof" followed by a thud. And then another grunt and thud. And then I heard it—the bloodcurdling warrior's yell from my nightmare.

I opened my eyes. Once again, the world slowed down. Maybe the slow motion was my brain trying to imprint these new memories so that I would never forget again. Before me, I saw a vengeful, angry god wielding a bow. He felled five more ninjas with arrows pierced through to the heart before anyone understood what was happening.

Xu looked up, sword still raised above him. His gaze connected with Zane. I saw Xu's eyes narrow in recognition. He looked at Tres on the ground and then back at Zane. He turned to me and raised the blade an inch higher, preparing to strike.

But instead, he stumbled back and the blade clattered to the ground. An arrow stuck out of his shoulder. Blood seeped out of the fabric of his shirt.

For a moment, there was chaos, but I registered none of it. Zane hopped to the ground from the opening where the moon's pale light rained down. In the blink of an eye, he was before me.

He tossed aside the bow and withdrew a blade. It sliced through the steel at my heels and then my hands. He pulled me up into his arms, taking my face in his hands. His gaze gentled, and he exhaled a silent prayer of gratitude.

His breath tasted sweet and familiar, like a breakfast pastry from a sunny Sunday brunch. I wanted to curl up in it with a warm cup of tea and go back to sleep.

I thought he was about to kiss me. I wanted to tell him that now wasn't the time. There were ninjas coming up behind him. But his eyes weren't focused on my lips. They were locked on my cheek.

His thumb swiped across my cheekbone. His path was slick, and I winced. His jaw tensed. His eyes darkened. A storm raged in his irises. It was a rage

I'd seen once before—more times than one if I had a moment to be honest with myself.

He let go of my chin. From his belt, he raised a mace; the ball hanging from the end of the wooden baton had countless sharp, deadly spikes. Zane turned around. He held a dagger with a handle in the shape of an Egyptian ankh in one hand and a medieval club of death in the other.

He raised both as he advanced. When he lowered his hands, he wreaked havoc on the ninjas who approached him. They went down in a spray of blood worthy of any graphic novel.

There were still over twenty ninjas remaining. They scurried forward. Instead of facing them, Zane backed away.

He turned and approached Tres. Tres's eyes narrowed as he watched Zane's casual, unhurried approach while a horde moved in at his back. Zane's face was blank as he came to Tres's bound feet. His eyes were dull as he raised the bloody blade of the ankh dagger.

Even though I was free, I sat immobile on the altar. Deep down, despite the carnage before me, I still refused to believe that Zane was a cold-blooded killer. Zane lowered the blade toward Tres. A scream of protest bubbled in my throat. But it was drowned in the sound of metal against metal.

Zane's cudgel smashed through the bonds at Tres's feet. Then his dagger broke the ones at Tres's hands. Without a second of hesitation, Tres jumped to his feet and rushed into the oncoming fray.

I watched in immobile horror as the blood ran off both of their blades. The crunch of bones and the screams of death turned my stomach. From somewhere, I heard someone calling my name.

I turned to Loren, still on the floor. Seeing her lying bound and prone on the ground was what I needed to put myself in motion. I slid off the altar, grabbed a discarded blade, and freed her. Giving her a hand, I pulled her up.

Once she was on her feet, she shoved me to the side. She struck out her foot and caught a lone ninja in the groin. The man doubled over, and I made an offering of him with my blade.

Loren looked to the side, and her face contorted. I followed her gaze to see Xu struggling to his feet. Blood from Zane's arrow dripped from his torn shoulder. With the hand of his uninjured arm, he grabbed for the dragon bones. He took the one with my signature. He raised it above his head with a grimace and threw it into the wall.

The bone shattered into a million fractured pieces that rendered my name mute. Loren and I exhaled as though he'd knocked the wind out of us. Then the fool did something even stupider. He picked up the first bone that told this twisted tale. It was the bone Loren's father had discovered.

"You destroy my legacy"—Xu raised it above his head with one hand, and Loren and I gasped as though he'd pulled a gun on us—"then I'll destroy yours."

We raced into the danger zone. Loren went for the bone. I went for Xu.

Loren was able to wrench the bone from his weakened grasp. He let her have it, but he had other plans for me.

I had no idea where the blade came from, but I felt where it went. Pain I'd never felt before tore through me. I sank to my knees.

"If I'm going to leave this life for the time being," he said, "then so, too, shall you."

He pulled the blade out of my gut. The serrated edge was even more painful coming out. I nearly blacked out. But I kept my eyes open. I heard Zane calling out to his Nova. Tres growled at Xu to let go of his Theta. But they sounded so far away, as though they called to me from another time.

I knew neither one would make it to me in time. The blade glinted once more in the growing moonlight as it rose above my head. Before it came down, a cane struck out from behind me. It hit Xu in the gut, in the chest, and then in the neck in quick succession. He went down. The blade extended from Loren's cane and ended Xu's long life.

"That was for my father." She spat on his corpse.

I felt hands on me. I heard myself being called every name I'd ever signed on a stone wall, animal bone, parchment, or digital file. But I couldn't respond to any of them. It sounded as though someone was praying over me. I even heard the word *Amen.*

"You have to get her away from us so that she can heal. Go quickly."

I couldn't tell if that was Zane or Tres. And I couldn't remember anything after that. I wasn't even sure if I'd closed my eyes, but everything went black.

CHAPTER TWENTY-SEVEN

"When most people think of archaeology, they think of huge reptiles buried beneath the ground and great rulers hidden in triangular castles in the sand."

I stood behind a lectern at the National Museum of China. There were more than fifty attendees before me this time. No one took notes. Everyone's eyes were glued to the covered dais.

"We're not just uncovering physical relics of the past, we are uncovering the stories of the marginalized, the minorities, the underrepresented. The history books are written by the victors. But sometimes they lie. Sometimes they get the story wrong. Sometimes they leave out the details."

I winced as I leaned too far forward against the lectern. My wound had healed. The skin had knitted itself back together in a day. But a phantom pain remained two weeks later. It was a mental reaction to the ordeal I had been wrung through. The memory, the feeling, the details of those events were things I was sure I'd never forget.

"It is up to us as archaeologists to give these buried voices a second chance to be heard," I continued. "Their stories matter. All tales must be told, even the ugly ones—especially the ugly ones."

I looked over at the side of the stage and nodded to Loren. She winked at me and then pulled the sheet off the newest display in the museum. It was the two dragon bones that told of the rituals and sacrifices of the Xia Dynasty. There were others still being excavated from the Gongyi, along with a full exploration and cataloguing of the buried city and the pyramid mound.

The find had caused quite a stir when it was discovered that there was ancient Aramaic writing on the tablets. The historians were interpreting the writings as a retelling of the story of Jesus, saying the fabled River Goddess was Mary and the Xia warrior was Jesus. I did not offer comment. Instead, I fielded as few questions as possible and made my way out of the lecture hall.

On my way out, I spied the tall and lithe Mr. Li of SACH sidling up to Loren, who was ensconced in a group of experts and academics who had tons of questions about her father's find and his work. Loren turned her back on Mr. Li.

We'd both achieved our goals. She had exonerated her father. I'd found the truth. And, like it often did, the truth hurt. I headed away from the crowd and wandered down one of the halls, taking in the exhibits.

The current exhibition on display throughout the museum was a collection of state gifts given to the Republic of China as a show of friendly relations and cooperation. There was a sculpture of two porcelain swans resting on lotus blossoms from the United States of America. The people of Thailand had presented a teakwood carving of an elephant transporting lumber. My eye continued to return to the painting of a peacock whose tail feathers were embroidered with pearls; that gift was from India.

A painting called to my attention. A face like my own stared out at me. The woman depicted on the canvas was painted in fuchsias. The brush work in the facial expression, especially on the cheekbones, was incredibly detailed. It was a gift to China from France.

I looked down at the signature. It was signed Qi, which also happened to be the word for the number seven in Mandarin.

I closed my eyes and exhaled slowly. Wrapping my arms around my shoulders, I gave myself a squeeze, but a heaviness settled over my limbs. He hadn't tried to contact me at all. Not once in the last two weeks. It was the longest we'd gone without contact since the invention of the telephone. I wasn't sure if I wanted to talk to him or hear what he had to say. But at least he should give me the option to call him names, hang up on him, or cry into his ear. Instead, silence.

"Nia?"

Tresor Mohandis stood on the other side of the hall. I supposed he thought the distance would keep the allergy at bay. But I was all healed and my Immortal strength had returned.

"How are you feeling?" he asked.

"Like I just came out of a really bad martial arts film."

He didn't laugh. Zane would have laughed. Instead, Tres's eyes roamed my body, looking for signs of weakness. "You're healed?"

"Like new."

He nodded, continuing to stare at me as though he wasn't sure if I were real or not. His gaze softened, but his mouth turned down in a frown.

We stood there in silence for a moment. Until, finally, I asked him the question that had haunted my waking hours the past two weeks. "What happened? After...?"

In real time, the concern in his eyes glazed over and was replaced with a thick sheen of fury. "They're gone."

I waited to hear more details about the fate of the Xia people of the Gongyi. Of course, I knew all the ninjas who were in the cave that night didn't make it out. But there were the people in the city. The children who Xu had ushered upstairs.

"Gone?" I asked.

"All of them," he confirmed.

"But ... there were children."

I thought back to the festival in Beijing. The children had danced that horrible dance, but they were still just children. They had to be around the twentieth generation. They wouldn't live that long with their blood being diluted.

"You didn't..." I began and stopped, unsure I

wanted to know. Not certain I could handle more nightmares.

Tres's face was as hard as granite. I thought he wouldn't answer me. Then I was even more terrified when he opened his mouth.

"No," he said. "We didn't kill the children."

I closed my eyes and sighed.

"At least, not yet."

I opened my eyes wide and stared at him. My hand went to my gut. Tres's eyes followed the motion, and he kept his eyes there as he spoke.

"He said that's what haunted you at night—the sounds of the children screaming. He didn't want to give you any more nightmares. So we agreed to wait ... and watch them. The root of the problem is gone. Xu is dead, as are all his grown sons who came with him that day. We have identified the ones who remained, and if any of them—male, female, or child—raises a hand against you or any of our kind, we will finish the job. On that, he and I are in agreement."

Tres gaze found mine. The unyielding steel brooked no argument. I didn't offer any. But there was still one matter left. "What about the land?"

He smirked, the hard veneer from a second ago

cracking. "I'm moving forward with my plans. I've let you win long enough."

My entire face tightened as I narrowed my line of sight on him. "Let me win?"

He grinned at my indignation. It wasn't a friendly grin. It was the look he'd give a worthy adversary after a hard-fought battle. "I'm going to bulldoze the surrounding forests and build a spa—a youth and rejuvenation spa." His eyes twinkled with mirth.

Wow, so he did have a sense of humor. He was going to build a spa for people looking to capture youth and vitality on a land that once belonged to people who killed to have it. Funny.

Tres studied me for a long moment before he asked his next question. "Are you going back to him?"

I knew what *him* he was talking about. I looked down to the floor, then back at the painting.

"You said the last time would be the last time." Tres snorted. The sound reminded me of a caged bull. "What power does he hold over you?"

I didn't know. I only knew that I ached to see him even now.

I crossed my arms over myself again, suddenly feeling very cold. Tres stood as still as a statue at the wall. When I looked up at him, another memory assaulted me.

I remembered him leaning against a structure looking at me just as he was now. His face was hard, but soon it broke into the most beatific smile. I saw myself run into his arms. He caught me, twirling me around and bringing me down for a kiss.

He must have seen the flicker of recognition in my eye because he pushed off the wall. Slowly, he made his way to me, as though I were a deer that would spook.

"Tell me about us?" I asked as he strode toward me.

"No." Tres stopped when he came within a foot of me. "I'd rather we start anew. A clean slate."

"Isn't the moral of this story that it's never a good idea to forget the past?"

He turned those words over in his head before looking down at me with those obsidian eyes. "Fine. I'll tell you our story, but only the beginning."

"Okay, how did our story begin?"

Tres leaned down and touched his lips to mine. Those hard lips were surprisingly soft. No, not surprisingly. I knew they were soft. I knew the texture of his bottom lip. Knew the shape of the divot in his top lip. I'd tasted his breath before. I saw all the memories huddled together in a balloon at the back of my mind. They were expanding, ready to burst. But then, he pulled away.

"If you want to know the rest," he said, "give me a call. I know you have my number. You've given it out to enough tree-hugging protestors."

And, with that, he swaggered down the hall and out of my life. For the time being.

CHAPTER TWENTY-EIGHT

The scenery along the roads in the south of France was beautiful this time of year, an artist's dreamscape of pastels. I pushed the pedal to the metal on the tiny sports car as I zoomed down the winding streets. I pulled up to the villa as the sun reached up to its high point in the afternoon.

Zane didn't stir when I came inside the unlocked door. He sat near the window before a canvas, his paints spread out before him. I watched him work in silence for a few minutes.

He was shirtless, how he often preferred to paint. There were smatters of the primaries across his toned chest. I watched his muscles flex and relax as he worked, just as I had done for five hundred years. The sight of his talent in motion still made my breath catch. I watched his fingers map out the details of my features just like he would do when he touched my body to bring it to a climax.

And still, my mind could not rationalize that the man I loved was the monster of my dreams. That he was the vengeful warrior who had brought death in that cave a couple of weeks ago and a couple of millennia ago.

"Zane?"

"*Oui, mon coeur*?" His voice was a soft caress, so familiar. I felt my body sigh at the sound of it. The warmth I'd been searching for, the jolt of energy, returned to my limbs.

He didn't turn to face me. His lip was raised in that perpetual tilt of amusement. But his eyes held sorrow.

"Did you break my heart?" I asked. "Is that why I went to China to be with Vau and Epsilon when...?" I still couldn't complete the sentence. It still did not seem possible that they were dead.

Zane put the brush down and turned to me. His hooded gaze narrowed. His long lashes shielded his eyes as he turned my words over in his head. When his eyes met mine, confusion shone through.

"Broke your heart?" he asked.

"Did we break up or something?"

He cocked his head and studied me from a different angle. I was used to him doing this, but not with bafflement coloring his gaze. "I have never left you ... not once in all of our existence."

His gaze skated over my body, but this time, his eyes lingered on the spot where the blade had penetrated my gut. I could tell he itched to see evidence that I'd healed. I crossed my arms over my belly and rose my chin in defiance.

"But you came after me?"

"*Oui.*" He nodded. "It's a good thing that I am obsessed with you." He smiled as he said the words, taking away most of the creep factor. "Both this time and two thousand years ago. Otherwise..."

His smile faltered, and he turned back to his painting. He picked up his brush and began adding detail to my hair. I watched him in silence for a moment, not sure what to do. Any other time, I'd be in his arms or wrapped around his torso.

"Ask me what you want to know, Nova."

"Because now you'll tell me everything?" I took a step closer to him, glaring at the marking on his back. "Even though you've known all this time."

"Now you are asking. Before you did not. You were trying to forget what happened. Why would I bring it up?"

I wanted to rail against his calm logic, if only to avoid asking the question that haunted me. But despite all the confusion and secrets between us, Zane still knew me well.

"You want to know if I killed them all back then?" he said, giving voice to my nightmare. "The men, the women ... and the children?"

His voice was so calm as he painted fine strokes. He turned to me when I didn't answer. His eyes darkened. Suddenly, I didn't want to hear any more. I wanted *my* Zane back. My gentle artist who never raised his voice, much less his fist.

He was right; I had wanted to forget. I had wanted to live in the fantasies he painted.

"I see that you remember the answer," he said. "I will go to any length to keep you safe, *mon coeur*. And if you doubt I would do so again, I believe it will take you another two millennia before you forget the most recent bloodbath. I'm only sorry that my arrow missed that maniac Xu's heart."

"Stop," I pleaded. I felt my body rocking back and forth. "This is not who you are. You are not some vengeful god."

"Who told you that? Tres?" Zane laughed, but he wasn't amused. "We are complicated beings, Nova. None of us are exactly who we appear to be."

"But you and I, we tell each other everything," I protested.

"No." He shook his head. "No, we don't. We tell each other the best things. What casts us in a favorable light. It has always been that way between us."

Now I wondered what else I didn't know about this man I'd loved for five hundred years. No. For longer than that, except I couldn't remember. Why had I forgotten? Was he not important enough for me to hold onto? Or did something happen that made me want to forget?

"There's something dark in all of us," Zane said. "But when I'm with you, when I think of you, all I see is light. I understand if what you feel for me right now is hatred. But, like I said, you are my True North. You are the idol on my altar, and I will worship you until I meet my end."

I felt the skin bunching around my eyes as I squinted at him, trying to find my Zane. "You can say pretty words, but they still don't change the fact that you lied to me."

"Do you wish me to tell you everything, *ma petite*?" He set the brush aside again and turned to face me. Putting his hands in his lap, he raised his head like an obedient student. "Ask, and I will tell you whatever you desire to know."

It sounded like a threat. I shut my mouth and stepped back. He hung his head in defeat, as though he knew there was no other outcome than my walking away from him. It pissed me off.

"Are you just gonna sit there?" I demanded as I stormed up to him. "You're not going to fight for me?"

Zane's head jerked up, and he glared. A spark lit his eyes, like when he'd seen the scar on my cheek. "I fight for you every day," he said as he rose from his perch. "I remember every day with you. All of them, for centuries and millennia. I remember every detail, every second since the very first time I saw you."

"You do?" And, with that, I deflated. I wasn't sure if it was from the pretty words aimed at my heart, or if it was from my curiosity aimed at my head. For someone who studied history, finding a living specimen of record was a watershed.

Zane deflated, too. But his chuckle was more sad than amused. "I know you better than you know yourself. I know you'll forgive me one day. It could be a year from now, or it could be a century. It could be more." He shrugged as he turned and walked away from me. He went to stand at the window and looked out at the pastoral countryside. "I am a patient man. I've watched civilizations rise and fall while I've waited for you to return to me. And during each of those times, while I remembered every bow you've worn in your hair, every smile you cast my way, every word you've said to me, you forget me again and again."

The desolation in his face broke something inside of me. I'd never seen Zane in despair. Annoyed—yes. Angry—check. Sad—yeah. But never defeated. I didn't like it.

It felt like he was being ripped from me even though he was standing right before me. It terrified me. I had him in my arms in two steps. But somehow, I wound up wrapped up tight in his embrace.

He buried his face in my neck, inhaling my scent. I pressed my cheek against the side of his head, getting lost in the curls of his hair. His body pressed against mine was so familiar, so right—even now, when I wasn't sure who this man was.

"Don't ask me to say I'm sorry," he said. "I won't ever apologize for saving your life."

I didn't. I wanted to live.

"Stay with me," he said. "We can stay here. I'll buy this place. Or we can live on your island."

I pulled away. "You know about my island?"

Zane brushed his thumb across my cheekbone. "I know just about everything about you, Nova. More than you know yourself."

I stepped out of his embrace. He let me go, curling his hands into fists at his side. The cold and heaviness instantly returned to my limbs.

"How many times have we done this?" I asked. "Broken up and gotten back together?"

He took a breath, and when he answered me, I wished he hadn't. "Eight."

"Eight times?"

He nodded. "Since the beginning."

"The beginning? *The beginning.* You remember *the* beginning?"

He shook his head. "I remember the first time I saw you. That was my beginning."

Taking another step back, I sucked down a deep breath. I stared at him, eyes wide and lips parted. "Tell me."

"No," he said with a small grin as he shook his head slowly.

I huffed and put my hands on my hips. "You said you would tell me anything I wanted to know."

He nodded, quirking an eyebrow. "And I will, in time. I'm smart enough to know that what I have in my possession is a carrot. And I know when to dangle it to get what I want."

I sucked my teeth and glared at him. But I had to admit, he truly knew me well.

"I don't want you to run again," he said, "like you always do. I want you to stay and talk to me. I want to work it out. We could go to couple's counseling, even. However long it takes, even if we become as weak as humans, I don't care. Just don't leave me."

The irony wasn't lost on me. Just a month ago, I would've jumped at the chance to spend an eternity with this man, even if it killed me. I looked at him now, and I didn't know who he was. I didn't know who I was.

Zane closed his eyes, as though he saw the verdict written across my face. He pulled me to him gently, not forcefully. He didn't kiss me. He rested his cheek against mine.

I closed my eyes and breathed in the familiarity of him. He called me his True North. But the compass inside me was going haywire.

He whispered in my ear, "Amen."

When I opened my eyes, he was gone.

CHAPTER TWENTY-NINE

All the fatigue was gone from my body. But I still couldn't get out of bed. My heart was a lead anchor drowning in thick, black sorrow. Even though the sun shone brightly through the window, I couldn't see the light of day.

Zane had left the villa two days ago. When I'd opened my eyes, the darkness had moved in. I spent my days in the bed, eyes shut, as I tried to call forth a past that continually slipped through my fingers.

The problem was with my hands, not the memories. The memories were all there, waiting for me to reach out and grab for them. It was my hands that were slippery. Whenever I tried to grab onto a memory, I couldn't hold on. I wondered if I actually wanted to know every detail of my past.

I sat up in the bed when I heard the front door click open and then shut softly. My heart raced as I sat still. I cleared my throat, preparing for the tickle. Did I hope it was Zane or Tres?

I didn't know. I just knew I was tired of being alone and wanted someone, anyone else, to focus on. I didn't cough. My throat remained clear.

A blonde head poked into the doorway before jerking back. "Damn, girl. For someone your age ... you look awful."

I closed my eyes, but my mouth opened and let out a laugh. My whole body was shaking with mirth by the time Loren plopped down on the bed. Something cold landed in my lap. When I opened my eyes, a spoon was held in front of my face.

"The cure for any bad breakup," she said, plopping open the tub of pomegranate ice cream. I took the proffered spoon and dug in.

"How'd you know I was here?" I asked around the spoon in my mouth. The velvety ice cream was heaven as it melted on my taste buds.

"Your ex." She shoved her own spoon into the tub and pulled out a heaping spoonful of ice cream.

"Which one?" I asked.

She smirked and shook her spoon at me like I was a naughty child and she was the all-knowing parent. "I knew there was something going on between you and Tres. I knew it."

"You may have known it, but I didn't."

Loren dug in the tub for another helping. "There are a lot of guys I want to forget. In fact, there are some that I *have* forgotten."

"Did he send you?"

Loren shoved the ice cream in her mouth, and I had to wait another minute for a confirmation. "It was Zane," she said.

I nodded slowly, scraping at the sides of the tub, scooping up the ice cream bit by bit. "Are you here to convince me to go back to him?"

"I told you in Beijing, I'm Team Tres. Broody Billionaire all the way."

"He threatened to discredit your father's work in those caves, remember?"

Loren shrugged. "He wouldn't be the first. But, at the end of the day, I'm on your side. For whatever you need. We can go and key one of Tres's planes. Or we can mix up Fine Frenchy's primary colors in his paint cans. Just say the word."

I chuckled as I stuck my spoon in the tub of ice cream and pulled out a heaping scoop, looking up at Loren before I put the bite in my mouth. Her eyes twinkled with mischief as she stared at me. Even though her eyes were blue, the look in them reminded me of someone.

"Vau was my friend."

Loren nodded and waited for me to continue.

"When she got her heart broken, I let her go off by herself to heal."

Loren nodded again. "I bet they hadn't invented ice cream at that time."

I chuckled softly, looking away. I should tell this human woman to leave, to not hitch her friendship to my wagon. The last real friend I had was murdered. Then I'd forgotten about her and moved on with my life. I was sure that broke so many laws of the Girlfriend Code. But alone was the last thing I wanted to be right now.

Loren crossed her legs under her and settled in like she wasn't going anywhere. She'd probably ignore me if I told her to go. And who knew what trouble she'd get into without someone at her back. I might as well keep an eye on her for a while.

"So ... Zane called you?"

"Like every other hour while you were recovering," she said. "Tres sent bodyguards to stand outside your sickroom."

I hadn't known. I didn't remember hearing a phone ring or people outside the door. I'd been trapped in my head the first few days, remembering things from the past. Then, when I woke, they slipped away from me again.

"Is that part of your superpower?" Loren asked. "Making men fall hopelessly in love with you, for like, an eternity?"

I shook my head.

"Can you fly?"

I shook my head again.

"So you don't feel pain unless you're around one of those two boys. Either one of them can weaken you physically until you get sick and die?"

"Pretty much."

"That's lame." Loren frowned. "And kinda messed up."

"It's very messed up when you think about it." I dug into the tub for another bite. The container was already half empty. Surprisingly, I was feeling a little better. "You only brought the one?"

"I can go get more," Loren said. "Or I have a better idea."

I gazed up at her. Her ideas so far had only gotten me into trouble. Still, my ears perked up.

"You familiar with the Eleusinian Mysteries?"

"The religious rituals centered around the Cult of Demeter?" It was a secretive group that traced its roots as far back as ancient Egypt. Its disciples believed the rituals they practiced in worship of the goddess, Demeter, would bring them prosperity in life, but more importantly, riches in the afterlife. For the most devout, it would bring rebirth.

I'd never found anything that made their claims credible. There had been a rumor of a tablet that depicted the rituals, or mysteries, of the cult. But it had been destroyed in the eighteenth century before I had a chance to take a look at it.

"What about it?" I asked.

"I know a guy who might be a part of the Cult of Demeter. He offered me an invitation. I thought he was cracked, but after my most recent adventure and introduction to the supernatural, I realize I may have been a little too hasty."

My ears were burning by the time she finished speaking. There was only one thing that bothered me. "Loren, how do I know this tablet that may or may not exist is not a forgery?"

She snorted. "Trust me, if I forged it"—she smiled sweetly—"you would never know."

My lips parted wider and wider until I was grinning. This idea had the makings of even more trouble.

Loren turned those innocent baby blues on me.

"So, Dr. Rivers, what do you say? Do you want me to run out and get more ice cream so you can mope over boys? Or do you want to go on an adventure?"

I stuck the spoon into the tub and scraped out the last bit of ice cream. "Sure," I said. "I could use an adventure."

The adventure continues as Nia and Loren
tussle with the Greek gods in
Demeter's Tablet
Book Two of the Nia Rivers Adventures.

Grab your copy today!

Lover of fairytales, folklore, and mythology, Ines Johnson spends her days reimagining the stories of old in a modern world. She writes books where damsels cause the distress, princesses wield swords, and moms save the world.

You can sign up for her mailing list and receive alerts and free reads at http://bit.ly/InesReaders.

The Nia Rivers Adventures

Dragon Bones

Demeter's Tablet

Templar Scrolls

Serpent Mound

Eden's Garden

The Misadventures of Loren

Spear of Destiny

Ring of Gyges

Hammer of God